TAKE A BREATH

A Collection of Claustrophobic Horror

Edited by Winston Malone

Storyletter XPress Publishing

Take a Breath: A Collection of Claustrophobic Horror is a work of fiction. Names, places, characters, and incidents are the product of each author's imagination or are used fictitiously. Any resemblance to actual persons, living or dead, events, or locales is entirely coincidental or made with the utmost respect.

2025 Storyletter XPress Publishing LLC | First edition

Published in the United States by Storyletter XPress Publishing LLC, an imprint of ISI Imprints LLC.

Hardcover edition ISBN: 979-8-9870046-7-8

Paperback edition ISBN: 979-8-9870046-8-5

eBook ISBN: 979-8-9870046-9-2

Cover art and design by Eoin Ryan

Edited by Winston Malone

storyletter.substack.com

enchantedbooks.shop

INTRODUCTION

This book comes during an era when safe spaces are offered, and trigger warnings prepare readers for potentially uncomfortable experiences. One would think that a collection of short stories centered around claustrophobia, an intense fear of enclosed spaces, might not be such a great idea. And maybe it's not (for numerous reasons). But the real world can be uncomfortable. Our daily lives can squeeze us in ways we never thought possible, with no end in sight.

When I was selecting the stories for this anthology, I rejected many deep-sea monster stories, not because they were poorly written, but because I didn't want it to be an underwater collection. Don't get me wrong, the "creepy, unexplored depths" stories have been among my favorites ever since reading H.P. Lovecraft's *The Temple*, and I even opened this book with one. However, I made sure to select stories with uniquely breathtaking horrors not often explored, if ever. This book has it all, and I'm confident when I say that by the end, you'll have contracted new fears you hadn't known existed.

The purpose was to explore discomfort and push beyond it. Safe spaces in these stories lure you deeper and don't let you leave. They shrink, their walls closing in until panic takes hold and bones snap. The only reprieve comes from the turning of the page, the compulsion to read on, to hope for the best.

Hope, prayer, wisdom, and bravery get us through the toughest challenges, that and breathing. Without our precious breath, we wouldn't exist. We must savor each one. Read on, and remember to breathe.

•••••••••••••

The featured authors deserve praise first and foremost for their efforts and patience with me as editor. A lot happened during the year this project was under development. I moved twice and opened a bookstore. This made for sporadic and often delayed email correspondence on my part. However, the authors stuck with me, and I'm thankful for their hard work helping me get this book across the finish line.

Eoin Ryan's incredible cover art and design brought this book to life in a way only he can. I'm consistently impressed with his talent and professionalism. He's always a pleasure to work with.

Thanks to the XPress Members who continue to make these projects possible:

Erica Astle, Peggy Boone, Kent Bridgeman, Thomas Bubb, Reina Cruz, Daniel W. Davison, Sarah Duck-Mayr, William F Edwards, J .M. Elliott, Mr. Troy Ford, Brylle Gaviola, hrl, Galia Ingatius, C.R. Langille, Joan Lass, Dave Malone, Pam Malone, Robert D. Malone Jr., Sandy Mariaskin, Jack Massa, Sandra Muzio, Danny O'Day, Leigh Parrish, Shaina Read, Ted Rorschalk, Richard Schultz, Cameron Scott, TJ Seator, skiddlzninja, Shifra Steinberg, Pamela Urfer, John Ward, Yvonne.

Lastly, if you purchased this book, thank you for giving our stories a chance. ~ Winston Malone, Editor

CONTENTS

THE LAST MERMAID

By Rose Biggin

WHEN AT LAST THE tides were deemed unlivable and the temperatures too severe to be sustainable and all the other creatures of the sea disappeared to some other part of the reef, they left behind a jagged cathedral, its sharp walls constructed from a near-infinite number of tiny sand-bones, its pale pinks and greens and flecks of gold faded to a sinister grey, its inverted spires plummeting down into the inky depths of the lowest waters, and where once there had been the echo of a thousand gorgeous songs, the soundwaves dancing languidly through shimmering light until they met a worshipping ear at their own leisure, there was now only silence, and where there had been the bubbles of a thousand frolicking tails, there was now only stillness. Nothing lived near the hidden reef where bones lay gathering sand, and in one of the chambers of this ancient coral palace, the last living member of the mer-aristocracy floats in her private parlour of pearls, above a bed that was once a magnificent clamshell.

She generally remains still, and although she is held by the gentle pressures of the sea, her posture bends at the back, so she has a stooped appearance, tired. Her hair floats out in impossible strings, thick and jelly-like—once a home for darting clownfish. Her tail hardly beats, for this can cause more scales to fall; her tail is tarnished copper where once it was the richest red-gold bronze, with patches of matted grey and dark green. She rises and falls slowly, steadily, regularly, just as a human would, should they have a tank to breathe from; her body clearly succumbs to some form of respiration, an internal part of her expanding and contracting out of respect for perfect buoyancy; but it would not at all be polite to examine behind her ears or beneath her forearms or the edges of her ribs for gills.

What preoccupies her in this crumbling expanse of ancestral coral? Her fingers clutch tightly onto something small.

She is not always here—she will occasionally need to feed, despite how efficiently she preserves her energy; on those occasions, she wearily kicks her tarnished tale to venture out onto the reef, moving her sharp fingers with deadly finesse through the silt until she finds something. (And anything will do; she has learned to cope with much, or rather little.) This coral-combing is not only an act of self-preservation but one of good practice: for any ancestral home demands its upkeep. As there are no longer shoals of uncountable triggerfish or other devoted chewing-things to do it, she must make her best efforts herself.

It is not quite true that nothing else is alive in this place, for what would a member of a vanishing class be without a faithful servant-fish? And so, there is a large and intimidating angler, a deep-sea hunter with a bulging jaw that is all angular teeth, a glowing bulb hovering on a tendril above its eyes. It does minor errands for her; of course, ushering prey into the palace used to be one of its favourites.

She lets go with her hands and two objects slowly, slowly tumble. Made of bone, a pair of them, carved or worn down into approximate shapes. This is what she does at the moment, most moments now; plays dice against herself, throwing pieces sourced from the remains of the extinct aquatic megafauna, trophies from a battle so distant she can barely recall it.

Her face does not quite suggest her great age. She would appear, at a glance, to be a very young woman. Wrinkles don't work the same way for her; she isn't drying out. But when she kicks her tarnished tail, she goes slowly these days, more than she used to; and if she tried to sing, she isn't sure how in tune she might sound, although she always had perfect pitch in younger times, measured against the whale songs.

The twenty-first century was an overfilled balloon; when its skin inevitably broke disruption poured out, spilling everywhere at once, things became atomised, the world was only pieces drifting; and, during this particular wave in the wake of ruptured time—this very moment now, in fact, just exactly as she casts the dice—a young post-doctoral researcher, who wishes to specialise in a particularly arcane set of pre-collapsarian methodologies of marine preservation, is putting an instrument resembling a large rubber fist into his mouth and falling backwards off the edge of a small boat he bartered for the use of the night before, feet splayed out like a starfish, his toes hidden by black flippers and his body and head wrapped in a wetsuit, with two huge tanks of oxygen, a pair of blue metallic cylinders ever at his back like supportive ancestors.

The diver conducts this expedition without the assistance of a research partner or even his former laboratory supervisor, for she refused to sign off on the trip, citing insufficient publication opportunities given the deadlock in respected maritime preservation journals regarding the existence of the mineral in question, nevermind its practical application, should acquisition be possible, which it almost certainly isn't.

He descends.

When the mer-aristocracy was in full flourish, our mermaid was at the very bottom of the hierarchy, her rooms scraping against the seabed, low in the palace; but we must be careful not to become lax upon learning this fact and interpret it through land-dwelling prejudices. The world of the mermaids ran upon the principle of greater depth equalling the stronger position; lower in the hierarchy was the place of one's social betters. And her bedroom, with its ever-yawning dusty clamshell and overflowing chains of pearls strung up everywhere, was positioned right at the bottom of the lowest turret. All of this is to say, it will need quite a dive to get there.

As light fades from the researcher's descent, he breathes in regular, slow, gentle rhythms, the sound magnified tenfold in his ears, constricted as they are by the tight hood of the wetsuit. With each exhalation, a small upwards avalanche of bubbles rushes to the surface, air going from where it can't be to where it must, and he drops.

When he reaches a pre-determined depth, he turns on his torch—the click loud in the oppressively silent water. Hand-powered, he wound the torch up on the boat, and he doesn't want to do it again, an indefensible expense of energy. The beam gives off a short, limited rectangle of slightly less darkness. He angles it downwards.

What does he hope to achieve, this researcher, as he sinks? He descends further, eyes ahead, trying to pick out shapes in the darkness that grows now beneath his fins, until he cannot see even his fins.

He is looking for a particularly rare thing. His research—and it isn't only his, to be honest, close to a dozen others in the laboratory, but he always felt he was the only one who really *believed*—his research proposed the continued existence of a rare material that might once have been found among certain reefs. That *were* certain reefs, the ones of stony sharp stuff and living bones, not the metallic megastructures his own world had to balance on. Beyond rare, broadly assumed vanished; he takes this plunge on the off-chance. It was all a guess, really, educated as it was. Various theoretical arguments were debated in the journals about its uses for purification or preservation, should it be found, but the more prominent voices in the field considered it nonexistent, never mind applicable.

A light flickers past him, and he jolts and almost drops his torch at the sight of a massive anglerfish moving slowly overhead. Its flickering bulb-light glints off its splinter-like fangs big as his fingers; this can't be real, it's too monstrous, but he isn't deep enough for the bends, surely? He holds his nose and blows, feels pressure readjust within his sinuses. He turns around and is face-to-face with the angler.

It bobs its head and up goes its tail; down once, and up once. Somehow, the crushing weight of the whole ocean has not squeezed out our diver's ability to read gestures, and he sees the very essence of a polite, even curt, butler-like nod. Its lightbulb flashes briefly off, then on again, and it turns and swims away, heading down. The researcher's eyes widen beneath his thick plastic goggles; the creature's meaning, *follow me*, could not have been clearer had it spoken the words.

When they reach the steeply plummeting inverted spires of the grand aqua-palace, the researcher's heartbeat is as audible to him as his breathing. He has found it; the stuff exists.

Coral!

They are wrong; everyone on land is wrong. Centuries of demolitions and the deepest dredging hasn't destroyed it, simply sent it lower. Or else this impossible construction, this deep cathedral of ancient shells and bone, has always been here, built by calculating minds to remain out of the way of even the most ambitious human harbours.

The anglerfish's tail moves casually, almost insouciant, as it leads him into a large open courtyard in the dense complex of coral. A visiting chamber of sorts; something between that and a great ballroom. The walls tower over him, curving inwards; kelp curtains, probably dark green but black at this distance, gently wave.

She is here and, for a moment, too focused on playing with her dice to notice what the butlerfish has brought her. She opens her fist and watches the small cube-ish bones drift on the barely-there tide, turning a bit as they drop, succumbing to something like gravity in their own steady time, and finally bouncing off the seabed in a small cloud of silt. Still focused on the bones, she gasps: her gills billow and stretch like a freshly-thrown bedsheet. For looking up at her, on each die, a single mark. She so very rarely throws a pair of eyes.

The butlerfish absconds to a discreet corner, where it will watch with only a blank expression of menace, its thoughts hidden by the hideous ambiguity of its skull.

She finally notices the ballroom's newest shadow and languidly turns her head to find the source, and when she first sees her visitor, her expression is so accustomed to remaining plain and melancholy her shock is hardly visible. But this only lasts a moment.

She gasps again, then kicks her tail to get closer to him, and the silty seabed hasn't known this much activity for generations: it spirals up around them, slow points of sand confetti.

She is entranced. The sheer accumulation of centuries caused her to forget the joy of this; although the sight is odd and unfamiliar, there is a deeply-known shape somewhere too, some strange beauty there. This new creature looks like a deep-sea thing, a thing of the trench; its skin is dark and rubbery, sleek and smooth—but oh, its eyes; those giant, hard outer eyes protecting the jelly-like window to the soul underneath. Even with its cheeks puffed out so obscenely—perhaps they are something it uses for storage—she is hit with just the right balance of novelty and the familiar, something new and surprising that tugs along with it the forgotten pleasures of things previously adored. The sheer beauty of this visitor, even with his strange mechanicalness and odd facial features, calls to her: it is a siren song (though she never knew any sirens personally) she cannot resist, and she realises there is an old story, as eternal as the grooves in the sand, always there no matter what individual grains shift and change and disappear and break, and she lets herself open to the powers of an ancient instinct: to love a sailor.

For his part, our researcher is now fully convinced he is hallucinating his way through a devastating case of the bends, that the deprivation of what his brain needs from its air has become dangerously—and he can only hope not fatally—unbalanced. He clings to some familiarities: he is kneeling on the seabed, he is surrounded by a mineral previously thought to be lost; he needs to take a piece of it back to the lab for testing, for proof, for measurement, for writing; and this creature in front of him, this strange floating figure with a human face, anemone hair and a burnished gold tail, shredded at the ends, is an anomaly in the experiment and need not adversely affect the procedure.

The walls of this coral palace are too far away; he cannot reach out and snap a piece off.

He breathes out, and the bubbles are eager to be gone. The creature before him follows their movement with some wonder, her gaze upon their rapid ascent until they become invisibly small. She puts an arm out as if to touch one, though it is too late to do so. At this gesture, the diver flings himself backwards (as languidly and slowly as one can fling oneself backwards while kneeling on a seabed) and she stops, her hand held out, with a new expression of shock and hurt.

The diver feels the injustice of having made the moment awkward. He looks down, as if seeking a distraction, and sees the ancient bone dice.

The mermaid watches him reach out a hand webbed by his gloves, and through filmy eyes, she watches him pick them up. She cannot call out to him: they are my last ones. They are all that remains of the world's last whale, worn down to this; they are all I have. She cannot tell him this, but nor would she; she would let him have anything.

The bone dice disappear into the diver's specially reinforced pouch for recovering delicate specimens. It takes him three attempts to close it properly, given how his hands are shaking; with his discovery, with fear, not of the mermaid or her deep-sea hunter companion with the sharpest of teeth, but fear that his mind will break before he can tell anyone what he has collected.

The ascent, then: he must begin. He looks once more at the mermaid, and she opens her mouth, as if to take a great, gulping breath, more than she'd normally take, more than she'd ever need, as if she needs to be more open, as if there's something she must force out of herself through her throat; her mouth stretches wide, as if in shock or surprise or to scream—her teeth can be seen, round as pearls, like soft stone worn down by an endless passage of water—and her eyes widen and the golden scales above her eyelids flicker, and she moves backwards, and flings her arms outwards, and lets them hover there, above her head, halfway between seduction and desperate surrender.

The diver kicks off from the seabed. He keeps his neck craned upwards, though his intention is not to ignore her. The carbon dioxide overload in his brain has him not knowing which way is up but he can cling to an old lesson: when in doubt, follow the bubbles.

When his hands bump against the high ceiling of the courtyard (perhaps it would be more respectful of mer-architecture to call it the low ceiling), he clings to the sharp surface long enough to establish a sense of solidity (while also feeling grateful to his gloves for their thickness). Then all sense of direction wobbles: the very idea of up and down turns somersaults within him; the needle of his inner compass breaks off and spins away.

He feels the whole of the seabed spread out below, curving inwards to envelop him, pushing ever upwards and forcing an ocean's worth of pressure further in, further in. He closes his eyes against the force, and a gap opens in his mind as if to cry out against the heady silence in his ears. And, as the ocean pushes from below, his hands press on the ceiling's scratchy surface, the only site of resistance. For a time unmeasured, he waits, trapped between the two, clinging to an idea—the size of a grain of sand—that he must wait for the feeling to pass, and have faith that it will, and not look directly into the long shadow of fatal panic sliding by smoothly like a shark.

The dreadful shadow passes, and with it, the paralysing sense of a fragile soul amid the entire ocean's weight. He opens his eyes; he remembers his purpose. Another moment passes, and the vertigo subsides until he feels he can make it the rest of the way, or at least attempt to try, or at least move on from here, to begin the attempt. The decision made, he feels stable enough to look back down at the mermaid.

She is lying on the seabed now, one arm above her head and the other across her body. Her tail is still. Her expression looks peaceful, as if she has been released from an exhausted greyness into something lighter. The anglerfish, in an act of animal vulnerability that's surprising given its stately deportment before now, never mind its unsentimental appearance, is gently nudging at her shoulder.

The diver shivers, then turns around and kicks out, following the spiralling architecture of the mer-palace until he leaves it behind and finds himself once more surrounded only by grey, dark water. He keeps kicking, and as the pressure squirms through his ears and into his mind he kicks harder, speeding up until the water takes on the silvery aspect, light reaching from... somewhere, and although he ought to slow down, the dimly remembered closing-in panic of before keeps him kicking, as if a dark beast burst up from the seabed to chase him, jagged teeth snapping at his fins. He forgets he can breathe, staring intently as he is at the flat paleness that can only be the surface while his lungs begin to burn, and he wonders if the paleness is moving farther away from him, knows it can't be, knows he mustn't wonder such things, wonders anyway, kicks harder, feels the inside of his head contorting with rapid changes in the pressure and keeps faith in his ascent while secretly suspecting it of betraying him until his head finally breaks the surface and he gasps out into the enormous dry sky.

On the boat, resting his back against the curving starboard side, breath still coming in heady gasps and a taste of sickly-bitter salt deep within him everywhere, he opens the specimen bag to examine the bone dice; his proof of the existence of coral. He reaches his hand into the pouch and cries out: a strange feeling resolves quickly into pain. Coral can be fang-sharp, after all, and he's cut himself, and after all the precaution. But when the sting fades and he's able to properly rummage in the bag, his exclamations turn to a more confused muttering, then cries of disbelief, then finally a vigorous round of swearing in all the languages he knows as he brings out handful after handful of useless sand. He frowns at the dissolved mess that is the remainder of his hopes. With his despairing head in his hands, he hears a new sound, from the specimen bag, or around the buoyancy equipment, or the oxygen tanks, or tangled in the rubber tubing, or out beyond the rocking edges of the boat... actually, he cannot place where the singing is coming from.

THE MAN IN THE HAT

By Hamish Kavanagh ~ "This story is dedicated to my fiancé Mollie, my first reader, however painful that role may be."

MY MUM TAKES CAFFEINE.

Grinding beans wake me up every morning. Percolating grinds greet me at the breakfast table. Lying to me with their smooth, chocolaty crema, sometimes I even catch tones of vanilla in the air. But I won't be fooled again. Three sips of that bitter shit send my fingers tapping, head screaming. Turns a bus ride to school into a wig-out. Convinces my body there are gunmen waiting at the other end for me. Morphs every cough or sniff I hear from the seat ahead into private sneerings about the way I'm wearing my uniform.

My dad takes alcohol and nicotine.

He can keep the first one. Not even the half-time commercials get me wanting a can to sip on. "Ice-cold beer on a Friday night. Will make the pretty girl wink and grow you three inches in height." Would be nice. I've just had to hide the car keys from a fifty-three-year-old man one too many times to buy into that romance.

The nicotine I get, though. Catch a whiff of that on the way home from school. Smell it on the breath of the French exchange student as she whispers something exotically cool from across the desk. I get it.

Both of them take Panadol on Sunday mornings. Drugs to offset side effects of drugs.

I take Ketamine.

Not every day. Just to get slinky at a house party here and there. Just to simplify the world down to two dimensions every once in a while. Got to be careful not to go over the edge and send myself into twelve dimensions, though.

It's a fine line. This is horse tranque at the end of the day. A K-hole is nothing to get cute with. But I know that and treat it as so. I'm sensible.

I'll be eighteen by the time Mum finishes the two bags of Colombian beans in her pantry, by the time Dad has to restock the triple dozen he's got in the garage fridge.

Drugs are drugs are drugs are drugs.

Not to them, though.

To them, there's a distinction between "useful" drugs, "acceptable" drugs used by productive members of society, and "useless" drugs used by losers, criminals, and drains on the system.

Solzhenitsyn argued, "The line between good and evil runs through the center of every man's heart."

My dad argued, "That man just needs a beer, a ciggy, and a starting quarterback who cares at least as much about the Patriots' season as he does about his new Nike sponsorship."

I humoured them, though.

After a close call during a standard term-end locker check and a strong warning from my headmaster (who just so happens to be a family friend), I deleted my drug dealer's number. Sure, that dealer is *still* my mate Wayno's older brother, and sure, he *still* lives above the garage band room me and the guys hang out in every Friday night, but it was a big step for me all the same.

I'm straight now. Strictly on the "useful" and "acceptable" track. California sober without the Whole Foods tote bag and all the name-dropping.

Straight is fine during the week. But straight doesn't get you invited to the parties. Straight doesn't even leave you with unfinished homework to keep you occupied.

All it gives you is time. A lot of time alone in your bedroom.

I've been searching through my dad's old records for some music I might be able to intro to my friends. Y'know, retro throwbacks? But most of it is so vanilla, so buttoned up in the world of the "useful" and the "acceptable." Don't know how he ever got it over on my mum. But I suppose they were meant for each other. Ironically enough, the few records among the bunch with any edge to them could really do with some help from a few drugs to lift them off the ground.

A guitar string bent beyond what I thought was possible, yet stayed in tune. A singer mused about time slipping away, waiting for things that don't matter, finding out about this too late. I'm probably half the age of the singer, yet I regret everything he does.

I've also been on TikTok a lot. I know it's bad for me. But it passes the hours.

There's a trend going around. I know. Ew. But I'm not learning a dance or anything like that. This one kind of seems tailor-made for me. Stuck up here. Alone in my room. In the land of the "useful" and "acceptable."

It's called the "Benadryl Challenge."

Step One: Take twelve to fifteen pills.

Hey, remember what my dad said? There are good drugs, and there are bad drugs. On the straight and narrow here.

After about twenty minutes, you'll start to feel drowsy. Dizzy. Kids, I don't recommend taking Mum and Dad's car for a joyride during this, by the way.

Step Two: Take a few more.

Aim to get yourself between sixteen and twenty-eight Benadryl. Relax, guys, don't tell me you're scared of a few numbers. This is an antihistamine, for God's sake! They give it to kids when they get a bee sting. Calm down. When we're out on the cricket pitch, Wayno gulps them down by the handful, eyes and nose streaming. They never seem to work, but hey, that's not a prereq for "useful" and "acceptable," so just relax.

Now, it's best not to try to talk too much at this point. You'll sound a bit drunk, well... maybe closer to someone who's just had a stroke. You might also forget where you are. It's best not to leave your bedroom if you can remember it's a bedroom. As long as headlights and horns aren't flying your way, I'd recommend staying put as best you can after stage two.

The internet will feed you a whole kinky sexual rabbit hole you might go down at Stage Two, but I'm keeping this in the realm of the "useful" and "acceptable." One thing I will note on this level, though, is forget trying to piss at all. Your junk will be out of order till you've ridden this out. You'll be so dehydrated in any case, so don't worry. You're not leaving your room to get water either way. I told you not to, remember?

Now if the walls close in, don't lose your shit. You chose this. If you start thinking about hurting yourself, spare me the angst. As if anyone would care you're gone. Your parents don't even know what you're doing up there. They've got their beer, their coffee, their respectability.

You think the RIP messages on the gram mean anything? You'll just be another reason for the school to roll out a D.A.R.E. campaign. Spare us all. Please.

They'll tell you seizures and coma *might* come next. And before you even start, eff you for getting disgruntled at *me* for leaving it till this late in the piece to drop that detail. If you're frothing at the mouth right now, spazzing out, unable to handle your shit. That's on you. What? You didn't think there would be risk involved.

C'mon. You take twenty-eight of anything, there's going to be risk. Besides, the coma talk is just a whole load of tracer rounds.

Don't assume you'll be able to tell though. Feeling like you're in a coma is kinda the goal here. Think sleep paralysis without the self-awareness. Your body will one hundred percent be frozen, and it will one hundred percent be filled with every terrifying sensation and hallucination your mind is capable of feeding through it.

But chill out. It won't feel like your body anyway. You won't even know what a body is.

So, while you're there, frothing from the edge of your mouth, eyes rolled to white, arms and legs flailing all over the place. Remember, it was you who got yourself here. You and your naïve, deluded little mind. Such a self-important little shit. Thought you knew better than Mum and

Dad? Hah. Quoting dead Russians to make your case.

Well done. You've made your point, and now you're never getting back there. The body that hosted you your whole life isn't even close to the place you're floating in right now. Now, all you can do is stare at your own closed eyelids and scream, "Wake up!"

And even if that works. Even if this doesn't top you and that biological shell does miraculously wake up. You'll never make your way back to it. You might be able to watch its movements in the third person. But if you think you're ever going to feel anything again. You really are delusional.

The hell you're bound for will have you begging for the detached curse of a life that they say psychopaths are all sentenced to. Those monsters might not feel any of the emotions we feel, but at least they seem to get something out of the power. Don't tell me Ted Bundy's glinting eyes when they arrested him for the umpteenth time weren't the joy of a predator living out all of its instinctive desires!

You'll never live again. Your future is going to be worse than a non-player character. Do you think the hallucinations are ever going away? Do you think you're going to see your wedding day and recognize it as a wedding day? No, you're stuck like this, you moron. A wedding dress is going to mean as much to you as a string theory calculation.

Drugs are drugs are drugs are drugs.

Moments are moments are moments are moments.

And when you eventually stumble your way to the grave. Which, by the way, I hope takes a very long time—there will be no transition from life to death for you. You've got more of this in store ahead: nothing mapping to anything, nothing ever making sense, time meaning nothing, because nothing is anything without something to ground it in. So you're here forever, you stupid seventeen-year-old dumbass; this is your eternity, forever young and forever without an age because that's not relevant to you anymore. You're beyond the point of relevance. You need a life for relevance.

Step Three: Pick a god, any god.

You'd be so lucky to see him. But if you do. If you're one of the many. I'll say a prayer for you.

He recognizes none. Some call him God. But the man in the hat looks like no entity to be worshipped.

He's the old hag. He's Der Grobman, The Tall Man, Slender Man, Slovoi, Domovoi, the Grim Reaper.

He whispers a language spoken by no culture. You'll never understand a word of it. But you'll know with aching certainty. He is Fear itself.

He is faceless. He is eternity. He is a burden on everything and everyone. Those people you can't remember will now feel pain because you've introduced him into their lives. He is in them as he is in you. He is you, and you are a plague on everything you've loved. He'll let you feel love for one final moment just so you can know it's about to be taken away.

He'll return your relevance just so you can tear apart the lives around you as well as your own. He'll let you be it and see it but won't let you stop it.

You can see him, can't you? You can hear his whispers.

The brim creeping into the periphery of this room, this stratosphere. The chill of his proximity. Fear pulsing out of his eyes.

Stupid boy.

You're his now.

And what's that? Someone on the stairs? Slippered shoes. Someone else calling your name.

Don't listen to him. Don't do the things he's telling you to do. Not to her.

Please.

Not to that sweet voice. That warm tone.

"Henry! One guess why our hallway smells like fresh lasagna? Dinner's ready."

The name lovingly given to you. Back when it was all safe. When all the confusion of your early life went away with a kiss on the forehead and your intro to the unconditional when she wrapped you in a warm blanket. Can you still remember that soft sky-blue fleece? Your brain might not, but your body does. You looked up and saw her kind eyes, that smile. A smell on her breath that was slightly bitter but pleasant because it was hers— you were practically still a part of her at that point.

"Henry!"

Don't do it. Don't listen to him. Do it to yourself. Be pathetic, that's in you. That's on you. You can't help that. But don't do this. Not to her. Don't bring her into his world.

The man in the hat does not negotiate.

Step Four: No one writes this part down.

THE MEDUSA

By Clark Boyd

I HOLD THE TROWEL high before driving it down into what's left of the Earth.

These are dark remnants we squirreled away before the Cataclysm, a few dense clods that we try to nurture in our floating sanctuary, the Osgood Habitat. Every day, it's my job to gather what the good doctor calls, generously, "The Harvest."

Today's haul: twelve potatoes, a handful of half-ripe tomatoes. One lychee.

I hate lychees, but I hate our dwindling freeze-dried ration packs even more.

A voice sing-songs its way from two rows over. "Aren't lychees the *best*?"

Jerome works with me in the Greenhouse. He has a carefree way about him now, courtesy of the Implant. He never angers, never tires of the repetitive motions suggested by Dr. Osgood's Agricultural Progress Mantra: "Dig, Plant, Water!" Outside this room, the reality on board is more like "Scavenge, Barter, Steal!" Pre-Implant Jerome came up with that, not me. He's also the one who nicknamed this space station "The Medusa" not long after we arrived. Since being fitted with the Implant, though, my gardening partner's withering (but much-appreciated) sarcasm has disappeared. He never looks out of the tiny porthole in the Greenhouse anymore, never seeks a single visual reminder of the brown rock that floats out there, utterly lifeless, the husk of a planet we once called home.

"Every day above ground is a good one," Jerome says. That's the Implant talking. Jerome used to hate this dank, cramped room.

"How do you figure?" I fire back.

He smiles and adjusts a glove. "Dr. Osgood makes the unlivable livable."

That's a matter of debate, but I'm not up for it today. Instead, I pick up a handful of soil and take a deep breath. I remember my simple garden on Earth, the fresh air. It wasn't much then, but would be a luxury now. Outer space, it turns out, offers very little personal space.

"You'll see," says Jerome. "After you get the Implant."

"I'm still not sure I want it."

Jerome shrugs, smiles. "I can't imagine life without it."

I'm sure that's true. Pre-Implant, I stopped Jerome from plunging a trowel into his neck on more than one occasion. Another time, I caught him eating handfuls of fertilizer and muttering, "Here's your growth model, Osgood." These days, though, he beams in triumph like a crazed prospector every time he hauls up so much as a limp carrot. Talk about Fool's Gold.

The device in my pocket beeps. I brush off my hands and check the screen.

"Therapy. 0900. Don't forget. Kisses."

Kisses? That's new.

Harriet is my wife. A while back, she had a four-month stretch in which she refused to leave her bunk. She'd barely talk to me, let alone send me kisses. "A little touch of space madness." That was Dr. Osgood's trenchant diagnosis. The only solution, of course, was the Implant. Harriet has won Orbiter of the Month for three weeks running now. Her face is locked in a giant smile at all times, and every day she tells me she can't wait to finish work and spend her free time reprogramming the composting toilets.

"You have therapy in ten minutes," Jerome says. "Harriet wanted me to remind you."

As I put my gloves away, I wonder what other silent messages they send each other via their Implants. The misting machines kick in and the atmosphere becomes even thicker. I can't see the walls of the Greenhouse, only the spindly vines of the pole beans directly in front of me.

"Dr. Osgood wishes us a pleasant day. He will see you in nine minutes."

Day? There are no "days" up here. I make my way towards the door.

"Eight and a half minutes, now."

I look back. Jerome waves and points at his temple.

"When you get your Implant, Will, we won't even have to talk!"

Yes. Won't that be something?

"Thanks, Jerome," is all I say.

I step out of the Greenhouse mist and into the corridor. Here it is dry, white, and sterile. Long lines of mirrors give the illusion of space. In reality, I can hold out both hands and touch the walls. Behind me, three little robots stand at attention. Their job is to sweep up any precious scraps of dirt that fall from our shoes and clothes and return them to the Greenhouse. Jerome and I named these Reclamators Moe, Larry, and Curly. They embody Dr. Osgood's unwavering belief that technology, *his* technology, can and will save humanity, one small piece at a time. Which is good, I guess, considering small pieces are all that's left.

The Stooges' brushes begin to whirl. I guess that's my cue to start walking.

As I make my way along the corridor, I find myself humming an old Pogues' tune that Jerome once loved to sing aloud. Something about starving sailors on a half-sunken life raft fighting for survival amid the tempest of a vast, merciless ocean. An aptly cruel melody, served up with lyrical splashes of cannibalism and unanswered prayers—The Medusa.

I remember, now.

There were once four Reclamators, before Jerome smashed Shemp against the wall in this corridor as he headed off to get his Implant. "One less Stooge," he raged as I tried to stop him from eating the robot's servos. "One. Less. Stooge."

•••••••••••••

Dr. Osgood and Nurse Richter are waiting for me in the Wellness Workshop.

"And how is Hilary?" Dr. Osgood asks.

"Harriet."

"Yes, sorry. Harriet."

"She's... a bit more smiley than before. I feel like I hardly know her anymore."

"Good to hear it. She was always one of my top employees back on Earth."

"You're lucky she got a plus one!" Nurse Richter says, raising an eyebrow at me.

It's true. I'm only here because of Harriet, and she was deemed "essential personnel" in the run-up to the Cataclysm, which meant two confirmed seats aboard one of Dr. Osgood's transports when the time came. Not even Harriet knew, though, that her billionaire boss had been secretly building The Medusa, or that he saw all of us as the pioneers of "A New Life in Space... for the Human Race!" Those were the exact words above the airlock as we boarded the space station. Pre-Implant Jerome used to wonder, often and out loud, just how long Osgood had been prepping for the end of the world. Or, indeed, just what role he and his technologies played in bringing about said end.

Just before he got the Implant, he'd started calling Osgood "The Architect of Our Doom."

I try, not entirely successfully, to shake these thoughts out of my mind as I stare at Dr. Osgood, resplendent in his white coat, a rictus grin stretching the corners of his mouth.

"So, what's the plan today?" I ask.

"Strip," he says, turning and walking away from me.

Nurse Richter picks up the grunt work as I start undoing buttons and snaps. "It's a little something called Virtual Exposure Therapy," she says, producing a long needle from the folds of her lab coat. Inside the syringe, a purplish liquid pulses and froths with tiny, rabidly gyrating creatures. "Dr. Osgood's patented nano-formula will read your mind's darkest fears and construct a scenario that helps you confront them. Facing your terror here in the Workshop allows you, Will, to become a more productive gardener, a more stable and caring husband, and, overall, a much healthier Orbiter. Eventually, I mean."

I lie back on a nearby gurney, and the nurse places cold electrodes on various parts of my naked body. I open my mouth in protest.

"Don't be scared," Nurse Richter assures me. "It's all in your head!"

Dr. Osgood's disembodied voice echoes around us: "William Braithwaite. Trial One."

Without warning, the nurse plunges the syringe deep into my upper arm and empties it.

"Sweet dreams, honey."

Her words slither into my ears as the liquid hits home, and my eyelids flutter.

The bright lights of the treatment room give way to a near-impenetrable darkness; the hospital odors are gone, and I smell damp earth laced with something equal parts sweet and rotten. I can no longer move. Every muscle in my body feels like it's frozen. From somewhere far away, I hear a voice.

"Give him ten cc more."

I'm at the edge of a six-foot-deep hole. An invisible hand pushes my shoulder, and I feel myself falling, turning over and over as I go down, bouncing off the dank walls, until I land face-up at the bottom. It's an extremely tight space. I'm boxed in on all sides. I smell rotting wood. Pine.

I'm not alone.

"This is interesting, Lucille. Another five cc should do it."

A sharp pinch, then suddenly a wooden lid descends over me. I struggle to open an eyelid. Nurse Richter smiles down at me through the ever-tightening crack of light. I smell perfume—lavender, perhaps, or rosemary. I shift my one functioning eyeball to the left. Gray skin, stretched like leather over a caved-in skull. The lace bodice of a wedding dress. Harriet's wedding dress. I see stalks of dead flowers held in a bony hand, hairy spiders jumping from her arms to mine.

Both women vanish when the lid slams shut. I'm in complete darkness. There's the faint sound of laughter and then I hear dirt hitting the top of the lid.

I've been buried alive in my own wife's coffin, it seems.

The purple liquid works as promised. It may be all in my head, but I can feel drops of cold sweat snaking their way down my cheeks, and every last feeler of a millipede as it crawls across my forehead. As the paralysis gradually wears off, I wiggle a metaphysical toe, then a finger, a hand, and eventually a whole arm. There's nowhere for my limbs to go. I close my eyes and take deep breaths. "It's just a dream," I say to myself. But when I try to open my eyes again, I feel my lashes gently scrape against the top of the pine box. That's when I scream.

"Adjust the sensors near the groin and amygdala, please, Lucille."

I find just enough space to bring my fist up to shoulder level and pound against the coffin lid. The rotting wood finally yields, sending a shower of dirt down onto my face. When I turn my head to the left, I get a mouthful of my corpse-bride's brittle curls. Now I'm spitting equal parts earth and hair. Motivated by an overwhelming dread, I continue to pound at the wood, ignoring the streams of blood I feel trickling down my knuckles. Eventually, I get a hand through. I thrust it upward seeking freedom, only to grab at the dirt above, which spills back into the coffin. After what feels like an eternity, a fingertip breaks through into the open. Not wanting to drown in dirt, I stop myself from screaming in triumph. Instead, I use both hands to wrench a chunk of the lid away. Both hands work frantically to move the dirt up and away from me, to get my head above ground as quickly as possible.

I set my feet against the base of the coffin and push upward.

Nothing. I do it again.

From far away, I hear Dr. Osgood's voice. "He's almost made it."

On the third push, my head emerges into the dim light of a crypt. Coughing and crying, I look down at my hands, illuminated by a nearby torch. My fingers are mangled and bleeding. Against all better judgment, I rip off a swatch of Harriet's dress, wrapping the material around my battered hands. Then I push my way out of the coffin and feel my way along the slimy stones of the crypt until I reach the door, which is locked. I can no longer use my injured hands, so I back up into the crypt as far as I can. Then, I lower my shoulder and charge the door, yelling and praying the wood and rusted metal will give way.

Just as I am about to make contact, the door vanishes. I stumble into the corridor that led me from the Greenhouse to the Wellness Workshop. The light is so bright that I bring my hands up to shield my eyes. Amid the remnants of the dress, I count four fingernails missing. I watch as blood and chunks of dirt fall to the floor. That's when I hear a familiar sound and look down the corridor to see three small shapes moving towards me—the Stooges. They stop in front of me, sizing up the mess in their otherwise pristine corridor. I shrug my shoulders in response, which loosens more dirt and sends it tumbling to the floor.

Then one of them, Moe, I guess, speaks, "Why I oughta..."

That's when I remember it's all a dream, and I laugh as the scene finally dissolves.

•••••••••••••

I'm still giggling when I awake on the gurney.

Nurse Richter isn't laughing, though. She rolls me over and jams another long needle into the base of my neck. "Got it, Seymour," she says. Groaning, I flop onto my back. Dr. Osgood's clean-shaven face towers over me. Odd, considering none of us have seen a razor for almost a year. On his dimpled chin, there's a tiny spot of blood. Impulsively, I want to offer him some of the wedding dress I think is still wrapped around my hands.

"Well, Breezeblock," Osgood barks, "you've finally faced your fears."

"It's Braithwaite. William Braithwaite."

"Hilary's husband. Yes, I know. She's amazing. Took the Implant so well."

"The only way out is through," pipes in Nurse Richter from across the room. She's feeding some of the fluid she took from my spine into a machine.

"Lucille—Nurse Richter—is only partially correct, William," Osgood says.

"What do you mean?" I ask.

"Choices, Will. Despite the somewhat... constrained... life here on my Orbital Habitat, I like to think my people still have choices."

"No one calls me Will. Not even Harriet."

He ignores me and presses on.

"Nurse Richter is running a series of tests on your spinal fluid. From that, we'll develop an Implant specifically designed to quell your fears and make you a happier, more productive member of our community. Spaces will seem more open. Your wife will feel more alive, more vibrant to you. Familiar, again. You will, I assure you, no longer complain about the hours you spend elbow-deep in Greenhouse muck. I'll even throw in a brand new trowel to sweeten the deal. Life will be easier. For all of us."

"You said there were other choices?" I ask.

"Oh, well, Nurse?" She sidles up beside Osgood, clutching her giant needle. "Refuse the Implant, and we'll force you to come to the Wellness Lab every day for a therapy session. Lucille will poke and prod, inject and extract, until we've worked through all your issues to my satisfaction. I should warn you that it may take some time, as your case seems quite complex."

"Jesus wept," I mutter under my breath.

"I'm sure he did," says Nurse Richter. "But *you* never have to cry again."

"Can I have some time to think about it?" I ask.

Dr. Osgood smiles. "Take all the time you need, Will. Now, get dressed, my boy. The Harvest awaits! Remember, though, your next therapy session is at 0900 sharp tomorrow." As I gather my clothes, his bony hand grips my shoulder, his long nails dig into my bare flesh. He leans close and whispers in my ear. "And whatever your choice, my dear boy, understand this: I never want to hear you call my beautiful space station 'The Medusa' again. Off you go."

I'm shaking so badly that I can barely get my clothes back on.

I stagger into the corridor, and the door to the lab slides shut behind me. Moe, Larry, and Curly are waiting for me there, ready to clean up whatever messes I've made, or, maybe, whatever messes I'm about to make.

My device pings twice.

The first message is from Jerome: "The Implant, buddy. Just do it!"

Buddy?

The second is from Harriet: "You'll never be free, Will, until you get the Implant."

Will?

Suddenly, the corridor shrinks. The mirrored walls close in and I'm surrounded by a million sordid reflections of myself. I put both hands on the wall to keep from falling. Dark flecks are beneath my fingernails, but I can't tell if the dirt is from the Greenhouse or the grave-digging session in the Wellness Workshop. Is this a hint of that old space madness? I have the urge to go back into Dr. Osgood's lab and beg for my Implant, to ask him to put it in right now and free me from all this, to tell him I, too, want to be Orbiter of the Month.

But then I remember that we don't have months anymore, or days, or lives we can even remotely claim as our own. The Implant is yet another trap.

So the real choice comes down to left or right.

Right leads back to the Greenhouse, my "buddy" Post-Implant Jerome, and whatever version of Harriet exists now. Not to mention endless sessions spent digging myself out of a virtual grave under the drug-fueled influence of that diabolical duo, Osgood and Richter.

Left leads... where? To an escape pod? To a cryogenic freezer that might keep me in stasis until we colonize the Moon or Mars? Pre-Implant Jerome always swore that Seymour and Lucille had some way off The Medusa if it all went south. Or—and this is the most likely scenario—left leads back to the airlock and a one-way trip into the uncaring vacuum that surrounds this space station.

I stand still for a moment, taking a few breaths of stale, recycled air. Through the porthole, stars twinkle in the darkness. The only way out is through, or so I'm told. It's time to find a life raft off this sinking ship, or die trying.

Either way, there will be one less Stooge around.

As I take my first step, I swear Curly mutters, "Ah, a wise guy... nyuk, nyuk, nyuk."

SHIKI-NO-KAMI

By Leigh Parrish

THEY'D NEVER MAKE IT in time. It was nearly a kilometer to the shelter, and the narrow streets were choked with evacuees. Michiko knew it, could see their fate in the glow of flames on the horizon, but still she pressed on. The wail of the sirens drowned out all other sounds. All thoughts other than the most immediate. People pushed mutely past her on either side as if somehow unaware of the baby strapped to her back. There could be no room for compassion here—only the ruthless demands of survival.

Even in the chaos, she caught movement out of the corner of her eye. A person in the nearby alley was waving, trying to catch someone's attention. Probably a child, based on their height.

The western-style cap on his head suggested a boy. He must have seen who he was looking for because he frantically gestured for them to follow.

"Hey, miss!" the boy shouted.

She glanced back over her shoulder, wondering how she'd heard him so clearly.

"Yes, you with the baby. Please come with me. There's a shelter nearby."

He was talking to her, no doubt about it. But why? She looked at the other people around her, still headed towards the public shelter as if they hadn't heard him. It was probably because of her daughter. At least there was someone with pity left for a stranger.

"This way, everyone," she shouted. "He says there's another shelter."

The press of bodies slackened as she turned back towards the boy, changing course like a school of fish. At least they'd listened this time.

"Over here!" the boy said, staying only long enough to ensure she followed him.

Maybe it was folly to trust the word of a child, but she had few other options. Traditional wooden houses made the city a tinderbox, helpless against the enemy's bombardment. She knew the destructive power wielded against them, had seen the charred remains of buildings and people the last time the Americans struck. There weren't enough shelters, especially not in this part of the city. More sensible people had already fled to the countryside, but she'd spent most of her money just getting here.

They hurried through a maze of alleyways and sidestreets, each seemingly narrower than the last. The buildings here were old and unfamiliar, but everything was unfamiliar in such dim and lurid light. Several times, she looked back to see if anyone else had followed. Each time, she caught only a glimpse of distant figures trailing after them. The boy never slowed his pace, no matter how much she begged him, always keeping out of reach and apparently beyond the range of hearing, too. All at once, they came out onto a broad, well-paved road that she didn't recognize. This was clearly an old and wealthy district, so it surprised her how close it was to the cramped jumble of buildings they had just left. But then, she was still a newcomer to the city, looking to hide her shame in the anonymity of the crowd. The dim light revealed well-kept traditional gardens interspersed with the curved rooftops of a number of buildings. It appeared untouched by the bombings, although she doubted any of it would survive the night. She allowed herself a moment to make sure her baby was still fastened securely, then followed the boy around the back of one of the larger structures. There was a rough-hewn stairway lined with sandbags, leading down to an open metal door—a bomb shelter. Michiko might have cried in relief, but all she could do was follow him down the steps and into the darkness beyond. She looked back over her shoulder as she crossed the threshold. No one was following them.

The boy moved to shut the door, but she stopped him.

"We need to wait for the others."

"There are no others."

"I saw a few more people behind us."

"Even if you did, we cannot wait for them. The fire is spreading too quickly."

His tone was strangely authoritative, unlike any child she had ever heard. She looked out into the garden, with its stylized pine trees spreading broadly over a picturesque bridge. No one else was there. She sighed and allowed him to close the door. If by some chance the others found this place, she would let them in. There was a faint click as the garden and the fire beyond it were both shut out.

The shelter was small, sized to fit a few people and no more. The corrugated metal walls had been painted olive drab, and the floor was plain dirt. There was an empty shelf on the back wall, and the light bulb above shed a dingy light that never touched the corners. The boy had already taken a seat on a bench against one of the walls. It was the first time she'd really had a chance to look at him. He was young—no more than ten years old—and was dressed in a schoolboy's gakuran[1] and a cap with a shiny brim. His hair was short, and he had a face that seemed both innocent and strangely knowing, like an old man reincarnated in the body of a child.

She took a seat on the opposite bench and began untying the cloth that kept her baby safely strapped to her back. Aiko had nursed earlier in the evening, but it was probably after midnight by now.

"Thank you," Michiko said, after an overly long silence. It was all she could think of to say.

He nodded, strangely solemn.

---

1. A Japanese schoolboy's uniform, modeled after western naval uniforms.

"Don't thank me. It's my master who brought you here."

"Your master?"

"He's the one who owns this fine estate. I'm only his messenger."

"And he sent you out on your own? Why would he risk your life like that?"

The boy shrugged, unperturbed by the danger he had been in.

"He didn't tell me. My purpose is merely to serve."

This was such a strange thing to say that she hardly knew how to respond. He spoke like some lord's retainer in an old folktale. She pulled Aiko onto her lap, wondering if she dared to breastfeed in front of this stranger.

"Who is your master?" she asked.

The boy smiled, revealing bleach-white teeth.

"A powerful man, from a family more ancient than the Kojiki[2] itself. It's an honor to be chosen by him."

Chosen?

---

2. One of the earliest works of Japanese literature, written in the early 8th century.

Something about that word bothered her. It made her rescue seem like more than just simple kindness. Like it was deliberate.

Time passed, mostly in silence. At last, she decided to feed Aiko, awkward and rude though it might be. Air raids could last for most of the night, and it wasn't fair to make her daughter wait. For a time, there was no sound but the gentle suckling of her baby and the muffled sounds of the outside. The boy showed no bashfulness or even interest in catching a glimpse of her bare breast. His gaze was impassive, as if he'd seen this all before. When her daughter was finished, she sat back and tried her best not to fall asleep.

"Where's the rest of your family?" the boy asked abruptly.

Michiko looked over at him, trying to decide if he was being impudent or just curious. His talk of her being *chosen* put her on guard.

"My brother and I were separated during the evacuation," she lied.

"And your husband?"

He smiled a little as he said this, like he already knew the truth. *Well, let him smile*, she thought. He couldn't possibly know.

"Dead. Killed in the war."

If only that were true, she thought bitterly. Last she'd heard, Aiko's father was still alive and well, enjoying the charms of some other desperate girl he'd won over with food and promises.

"I'm sorry for your loss," the boy said, a hint of amusement in his voice.

They had never met before. And even if they had by some chance, how would this child have found out her most intimate secrets? Daisuke might have been a lying bastard, but at least he was discreet.

"Who are you?" she said. "You don't talk like any child I've ever met."

"I told you. I'm just a messenger. That's all you need to know."

"Surely you have a name, though."

"It doesn't matter."

He got up and put his ear to the door, listening intently. She wanted to press him further, but he'd made it clear that he wouldn't answer her. *Maybe he didn't have one*. But that was absurd. Everyone had a name.

At last, she could no longer contain her curiosity.

"Why do you say that it doesn't matter?"

He glanced at her from over his shoulder. "Servants like me don't need a name."

Michiko stared at him, but he'd already gone back to listening at the door, as if he'd said nothing out of the ordinary. A better person would have felt pity for this poor, nameless boy, but she felt a shiver of revulsion instead. Looking at that blank, emotionless face, it was hard to imagine such a creature being born of a human mother. But then, she'd seen monstrous things enough in this war, all with a very human origin. Things she tried her best to forget.

"Namu amida butsu,"[3] she muttered, almost reflexively. It was a chant she learned as a child; a small comfort in an often comfortless world.

The boy laughed. A harsh sound, strangely guttural.

"You still don't understand why you're here, do you? Poor little fool. You'll never reach your paradise."[4]

"What... what do you want with us?"

He shook his head.

"What do *I* want with you? Nothing. I have no wishes of my own—only his. I'm an empty shell;

---

3. Often translated as "I take refuge in Amida Buddha" or "Homage to Amida Buddha".

4. In Pure Land Buddhism, a place where one can be reborn and trained to become a full Buddha.

a vessel of paper, to be used and then discarded. And my purpose has already been served. It was served the moment this door locked behind you."

••·•·••●••·•·••

The old man sat back in his seat, watching with annoyance as his driver slowly made his way around to open the door for him. All his best human servants had already been killed or drafted. What was left were the dregs; those too old or useless for the army to take from him. His paper servants were far more reliable, but there were some tasks they were unsuited for. Ancient means did not always work for modern ends. But sometimes—

The car door opened. His driver was young and looked respectable enough in his uniform, at least. It was only when he stumped about on that artificial leg that you could tell why nobody else had wanted him.

"It's a miracle, sir," he said as he extended his arm for the old man to take. "Most of the estate has been spared by the fires."

"I can see that for myself," the old man snapped. That wasn't entirely true, but he'd be damned if he'd let this weakling condescend to him.

The grounds swam into view, blurry but green amidst the scorched wasteland that surrounded them. He allowed himself a smile of satisfaction. The business with that woman and her baby was unfortunate, but the kami of this place had been quite clear in what they required. And besides, they were nobody, really. A peasant and her bastard child; one of many who had come to the capital seeking work. A necessary sacrifice, and one who would not be missed. His son didn't embrace the ways of his ancestors, trusting instead in glass and steel and petrol. But all the firetrucks in the world couldn't overcome the onslaught the Americans had unleashed upon them. In the end, there had been only the old ways and the ancient gods that they served.

THAT SPELEOBOX

By Rachel Henderson ~ "For my husband Price, who always keeps me company in the caves."

I DON'T REGRET BUILDING that speleobox.

I say *that* speleobox, not *my* speleobox, because even though I built it, it's not really mine—the blueprint came from the Devil's Reach Grotto in Wyoming. We don't have a grotto in Omaha. No caves, no grotto, no point.

Which is why I wanted the speleobox. It was bad enough we had to slink back to Nebraska after fifteen years away, fifteen years of freedom from cornfields and strip malls—the real problem is having no *escape* here. Caving is my escape—and may be the most important thing in my life.

I said those exact words to Mason after he lost his job, after he made the *unilateral* decision to sell our condo and move us back to Omaha, but he didn't give a shit. I wish he did. I blew so much energy trying to get him involved, get him interested, get him to participate—nothing took. Mason was never a caver.

If you're a caver, and there's no caving nearby, a speleobox is the next best thing. Basically a big wooden box, twelve feet by twelve feet, made of tunnels. Those tunnels should be varied—back, forward, up, down—crammed together like a honeycomb, so you get two, three hundred feet of squeeze space. *Squeeze* space, not *crawl* space. If you can *crawl* through the tunnels, you're not in a speleobox.

A speleobox should be so tight you feel like you're dying and being born at the same time.

I needed a speleobox.

Three months ago, I wrote to Devil's Reach, and their secretary sent me the blueprint. "Blueprint" was his word; it was more like a rough sketch. Practically drawn in crayon. They got the plans from a defunct grotto on the East Coast, he said, but never bothered building anything.

I bothered. I bothered right away.

Mason freaked when he saw the first load of supplies—lumber, screws, sealant, glue—and demanded to see the receipt. Every trip to the hardware store was a battle. Money was the issue, he claimed; we needed to save until he found work, he claimed; we were deep in debt, he claimed, but I knew the real issue—he hated seeing me get enjoyment out of something, especially something he didn't understand. And I wasn't about to let his little temper tantrums get in my way.

Best guess, it took six days to build the speleobox. I know I started on a Sunday afternoon and finished in the wee hours of a Saturday. Which Saturday, though, I'm not quite sure. If you could ask Mason, he'd say I can't remember how long it took because I was drinking too much.

Not disputing the drinking. Or the lost days. But the whiskey was incidental—*confusion* is what sucked those days away.

Like I said, the blueprint was crap. Whoever designed it needs therapy, medication, or Jesus. Possibly all three.

Its problems included:

1. Tunnels that dead-end, tunnels that loop back in on themselves, tunnels that, impossibly, do *both.*
2. Incoherent route, chaotic near the walls, concentric near the center.
3. Clear entrance—no exit whatsoever.

And these were peanuts compared to the biggest design flaw: the blueprint *wouldn't stop changing.* Extra tunnel here, disappearing turn there—one time I looked at it and, swear to God, the floor was gone. Not gone forever—not long enough to stop the build—just long enough to make me doubt my eyes or wonder if Mason was right about the drinking.

He was not.

Confusion sucked those days away. Six days, twelve, twenty-four, however many. Mason didn't offer help, *of course*. It was all me. I built that speleobox alone—and I built it well.

I made something beautiful.

Before even going inside, you can *feel* the speleobox—a heaviness travels through your torso, wrapping around your organs, settling above your solar plexus—and the air around the entrance is rich and buzzy. Comforting—whole-body anesthesia. You barely notice the first squeeze.

Squeeze may be the wrong word. More like—pinch.

Or scrape.

The scraping is a surprise, if I'm honest. I used thirty cans of varnish, made sure the wood was glass-slick before construction, but it's a different ball game *inside*. At least for the first few minutes, in the outer tunnels. Like dragging yourself across a cheese grater.

Once you're past the scraping, the tunnels change again.

I know I built them out of wood. I bought the wood. Mason screamed at me about the wood.

But Lord help me, those second-layer tunnels are soft. Dirt-soft.

It makes the journey easier. Some of the worst curves and flips are in those tunnels, where the ceiling drops to six inches in height. I find the best method here is to go headfirst, arms at your sides, frog-kicking your feet—the tunnel helps you along, feels its way around you, nudges you forward. The softness isn't unpleasant—a bit wormy, but also warm.

The warmth is weird. Very un-cave-like. It gets warmer the further you go, warmer and wetter, then the softness loses its grit and the tunnel *finally* smooths out—and right around this point it gets hard to breathe. What little air is left is syrup-thick—reeks of sweet cheese and sour, old eggs. It coagulates in your lungs.

If there's anything worth seeing in this inner layer of tunnels, too bad—you're blind.

You lose yourself completely.

As it turns out, the "no exit" problem isn't a problem at all. I've gone into the speleobox every night since building it, and every morning I wake up inside my house—sometimes in bed, sometimes on the couch, sometimes underneath the kitchen table. I'd double-check that I didn't miss a trap door or a hidden hatch if I still had the blueprint, but it's long gone. Don't ask where—it disappeared right after I finished building. I'd blame Mason, if I could—but this isn't his fault. Couldn't possibly be his fault.

It's just gone.

Exit aside, I wish I could have another look at the blueprint to see the dead-center tunnels—the *core* of the speleobox. I know the drawings were a shifting mess, but I need to stop this terrible, nagging thought that I've never actually made it to the core—*will* never make it to the core—because somehow I built the core for single-use, like one of those spring-loaded mouse traps. One mouse—one snap.

Perseverance is key. I'll try again tonight—tomorrow night—every night for the rest of my life if I have to. But the idea that I'll never experience the full *artistry* of the speleobox—the idea that something this beautiful was wasted on Mason—it's unbearable.

He didn't *want* to go into the speleobox.

He cried—I remember that. He cried when I pushed him toward it—babbled about love and leaving Omaha and how things would be different if I just put down the knife. He cried as he folded into the entrance—*folded*—like his bones were liquid. He cried the whole way through—back, forward, up, down.

Two months later, he's still crying.

That's the bad thing about the speleobox—the part I don't like talking about. It starts in the outer tunnels, a ways behind you, like an ambulance stuck in traffic. Eventually, it wraps around your ankles and slithers up your legs. The closer you get to the core, the further it moves up your body, little sobs tickling your skin, pressing against your neck, nibbling at your earlobes. By the time you black out, the cries are suffocating. You're in a coffin made of sound.

Mason didn't want to go in—but he didn't have a choice. *I* didn't have a choice. His name appeared on the blueprint, clear as anything, right in the middle. Not my name—his. And as much as I hate the crying, as much as it *kills* me that I may never reach the dead-center, I can still appreciate the fact that I built that speleobox—all by myself—and I built it well.

I have no regrets.

A SINKING FEELING

By Warren Benedetto

"HOW LONG BEFORE HELP comes?" Andrei asks.

We sit atop a sodden mattress, floating semi-submerged under the water. It isn't exactly a life raft, but it's buoyant enough to keep us somewhat dry. Without the mattress, we'd be in the water up to our necks. With it, the water is only up to our ribs.

Andrei's wet hair sticks to his face in thick, matted strips resembling rotting seaweed. Beads of water cling to his spiny, rust-colored beard. His chattering teeth remind me of the clicking of Scrabble tiles in a velvet bag.

"I don't know," I reply. "A few hours? They'll probably need to wait until the sun is up."

"But they'll come, right?"

I nod, trying to sound more confident than I am. "They'll come."

I know the ship has an emergency beacon. When triggered, it's supposed to send a distress signal, GPS coordinates, and other data to help rescuers locate the damaged vessel. If it worked, help should be on its way.

If it worked.

I have no idea what hit us. We were asleep when it happened. Both of us were thrown from our bunks, sliding across the suddenly slanted floor and crashing painfully into the opposite wall. I managed to stand and stumble over piles of fallen debris toward the cabin door, where I paused before exiting to peer through the peephole into the hallway. It was a good thing I did. Otherwise, we'd be dead.

An irregular gash, maybe 15 feet long, had been gouged through the hull outside our cabin. A torrent of water the color of graphite foamed in through the breach, transforming the narrow hallway into rapids roaring toward the front of the ship. The ship had turned nose-down, taking on water at an incredible rate. That could mean only one thing: we were sinking.

The descent was quick. At first, I heard the crew's screams echoing through the ship, overlapping with the sounds of rushing water and rending metal. Some begged for help, while others prayed or wailed inconsolably. Then, one by one, each of them fell silent. Even after the screams ended, there was still some banging, metal on metal, as if someone was hitting a wrench against a pipe. The pattern was unmistakable: S-O-S. Soon, that, too, subsided, growing weaker and weaker until it tapered off to nothing.

Andrei and I called for help until our voices were raw. After a while, we lapsed into silence too—there was no point in wasting our breath. Now, we sit quietly on the sinking mattress, each lost in our thoughts, waiting for the end.

I mostly think about my mother. She was an addict who used to go missing for days on end, taking off with whoever was supplying drugs at the time. She'd stumble home for a few days, burn a quesadilla or two in a halfhearted attempt at mothering, then disappear again.

Nighttime was the worst. I'd sit in the dark for hours, huddled on the filthy mattress in our tiny one-room apartment, waiting for her to return. I always left the door unlocked in case she forgot her keys. As I grew older, her absences grew longer. Hours turned to days and days into weeks. Eventually, I started locking the door again.

A few months after I last saw her, I found out she had OD'd in a hotel room in Arizona, 350 miles from home. The police found her with a needle in her arm and a baby in her belly.

I was twelve.

My mind goes there because it was the last time I felt so scared and alone. I had the same sense of powerlessness. There were no good options. No good outcomes. No matter what I might do, I was doomed.

The funny thing is, I was wrong about that. I turned out alright. I moved in with my grandmother, finished high school, took some community college classes, and ultimately found a life as a ship's cook. I knew being at sea was risky. Logically, that made sense. But I never felt like I was in danger. Until we sank, that is.

When the ship hit bottom, the hull let out a mournful groan that sounded like a whale song. Then, there was a series of bangs, one after the other, like a ten-car pileup on the freeway. A second later, the whole room turned upside down, sending Andrei and me tumbling ass over elbows. It was like being in a snow globe thrown from an airplane.

Our cabin is almost entirely inverted now, with the angle where the floor meets the wall steepled overhead. We're trapped in a triangular air pocket, maybe five feet wide and ten feet long, with only a few inches of headroom on our floating mattress.

Andrei's voice breaks me out of my thoughts. He sounds far away. Lost. Numb.

"Marla had her ultrasound last Tuesday," he says absently.

"Oh, yeah? Boy or girl?"

"Girl. We're gonna name her Ripley."

"Ripley? Like, from *Alien*?"

He smiles a little. "Pretty badass, right?"

"Pretty badass."

I look down through the murky water. I can make out the dim shape of the cabin door far below. An emergency beacon over the door frame flickers in the filthy liquid, filling the space with an eerie yellow glow that reminds me of a vintage horror film. The door was supposed to have been watertight—the damage to the ship must have deformed the frame enough to compromise the seal, allowing water to rush in around the edges.

Suddenly, a hollow *clunk* resonates through the ship. The water's surface ripples and sloshes, distorting my view of the door below. That sound is followed by another, one that my concussion-dulled brain has trouble processing.

"What was that?" Andrei asks. He looks around nervously.

I hold my hand up to silence him, then place my ear against the wall. The metal is cold and slimy against my face.

I don't know how long we've been underwater, but however long it has been, we haven't heard any noises outside of our movement and the occasional groan of the ship's structure as it settles into the ocean floor. But this noise is different.

Something is moving. And it's close.

I listen in silence for a few seconds. Then, I hear the sound again, louder this time. It's a dissonant squeal like a garden rake dragged across a glass pane. I don't know what's making the sound, but I'm not taking any chances. It might be a diver or one of those underwater drones with a camera on the end. Maybe we're being rescued. Maybe we've been found.

"Hey!" I shout. The sound of my voice is explosive in the enclosed space. I begin pounding my palm against the wall. "Hey! We're in here!"

Andrei balls up his fists and joins me, drumming on the wall as hard as he can. "Help!" he yells. "Hey! Hello! Can you hear us? Hello?"

We keep at it for a solid minute, making as much noise as possible. Then, we stop and listen. The water around us grows still. I can see to the bottom again, down to the door.

My heart sinks.

While Andrei and I were pounding on the wall, someone—or *something*—opened the door. Earlier, I could see a horizontal handle and crisscrossing support struts; now, there's nothing but a yawning black chasm opening into the lightless depths below.

"Andrei," I say quietly. "The door."

"What?"

"The door," I say again, more urgently this time. "It's—"

I stop mid-sentence, watching as a long, black appendage wraps around the top edge of the doorway from outside. It's featureless and so dark that it seems like a tear in the fabric of reality. Even the ink-black depths of the water beyond the door look pale in comparison. The thing snakes along the edge of the doorway, coils around the emergency light's plastic housing, and squeezes, crushing the fixture in its grip.

The resulting darkness is total. Not a single photon of light remains. I'm completely blind.

A loud sloshing noise follows the blackout, sounding like something moving across the water's surface. I whip my head around, trying to locate the source. I think it's coming from the far end of the space, past Andrei, but it's hard to tell—the way sound bounces off the angled ceiling makes every noise seem to be coming from everywhere at once.

"What was that?" I whisper.

"I don't know," he answers. "I can't see anything."

"You heard it, though?"

"Yeah." His voice is heavy with fear. "There's something in here."

My mind races as I try to picture what it might be. A shark? Maybe. But sharks don't have... a what? What the hell did I even see? A tentacle? No, not really. Tentacles have suckers on the bottom. What I saw was completely smooth. It was more like a worm or an eel. It didn't move like one, though. It wasn't slithering. Or swimming. It was *reaching* for the light. And then, it snuffed it out. It was intentional.

"What do we do?" Andrei asks. His breath comes in short, panicked gasps.

"Just don't move. Maybe it'll go away."

"But—"

"Shhh!"

I listen intently for any indication of where the thing might be. Is it under us, swimming along the bottom? Or is it slipping silently along the surface, circling us, winding in figure-eights as it tries to decide who to attack first?

I attempt to rein in my panic. The thing might be harmless—just a curious fish exploring the new artificial reef that has so rudely intruded on its habitat. I just need to wait until it goes away.

The water is calm. Quiet. There is no sound other than Andrei's labored breathing. There's no attack. No movement. No nothing.

Then, a voice speaks. It's smooth and pleasant—a woman's voice.

"Andrei?" it says.

My eyes widen. *What the hell was that?* Before I can say anything, Andrei answers.

"Marla?" His voice is full of awe.

"Come home, Andrei. We're waiting for you. Ripley and I."

Andrei exhales a shuddering sob. "I know. I'll be back soon. I swear."

"Andrei?" I say, on the edge of a total breakdown. "That's not Marla."

Of course, it isn't. It can't be. We're trapped God-knows-how-far under the ocean, dozens of miles out at sea. And yet, I hear the voice, too. It's as real as my own. As real as Andrei's. It even echoes off the walls of the space a little, just like ours.

There must be a logical explanation. Maybe it's some sort of auditory hallucination, a shared delusion manufactured by our oxygen-starved brains. Or maybe it's sensory deprivation—the darkness is so complete that our minds have started making sounds to fill the void in our senses.

"Where are you?" Andrei says to the not-Marla. "How are you here?"

"It doesn't matter," the voice replies. "Come on. Let's go home."

I realize that I can see again. The dark isn't quite as absolute as it was a moment before. A barely perceptible luminescence pulses underwater in the corner of the room, below the water's surface. It gives off just enough light to see Andrei silhouetted against the dim, blue glow.

It isn't an auditory hallucination—I can *see* his wife under the water: her pale, porcelain skin, her eyes sparkling like blue topaz, her black hair rippling behind her like a sheet of silk in a bath.

I can see the curve of her breasts and the roundness of her belly.

It's Marla.

She drifts closer to Andrei. He leans down to reach for her, the water up to his shoulder.

"Marla," he whispers. His tone is almost reverent.

"Andrei!" I hiss. "Don't—"

Suddenly, Marla disappears in a burst of brilliant, white-hot radiance. The searing light stabs through my eyes, blinding me, as the room fills with a terrifying screech. It's the same metal-on-glass squeal we heard before—except now, it's a thousand times louder.

I cover my ears and squeeze my eyes shut. Then, I open one eyelid just enough to see what might happen next. I wish I hadn't.

Light emanates from a fleshy orb attached to the end of a smooth black appendage like the one that had extinguished the emergency beacon. It protrudes from the center of a gaping mouth lined with rows of clear, crystalline fangs, pin-sharp and glistening. The mouth is at the front of an undulating, boneless body, midnight-black and lined with a dozen more eel-like tentacles. Above the mouth, an oily black eyelid blinks over a single enormous eye the size of a volleyball.

The light strobes, turning the creature's fluid movements into hellish snapshots of jerky, uneven motion. Its tentacles lash out of the water with whip-like speed, seizing Andrei and yanking him into its octagonal mouth, where barbed hooks prevent him from escaping.

The last thing I see before I close my eyes again is the creature dragging Andrei into that horrifying maw, his body folding in half backward, his spine snapping like a tree branch in a summer storm.

He never makes a sound.

•••●•••●•••●•••

I expected the creature to grab me after Andrei, but it didn't. Not yet, anyway.

As far as I can tell, it's gone. It'll be back, though. I'm sure of it.

In the meantime, I sit here in the darkness, alone and scared. Waiting. My eyes are open, but it doesn't matter. It's just as dark with them open as when they are closed.

Time passes. My thoughts return to my mother.

I'm twelve again. I'm sitting on the sagging mattress in our tiny one-room apartment, waiting for her to return. It's after midnight. The electricity is out. The room is pitch-black except for a faint blue glow flickering in the corner from the streetlight outside.

I hear her voice just beyond the door.

"Billy," she says. "I'm home."

I slide off the mattress and walk across the apartment, water sloshing around me as I move. I see my mother silhouetted through the screen, her black hair flowing behind her in mesmerizing waves.

I unlock the door. Open it. And step out into the brilliant, blinding light.

NO WAY OUT BUT THROUGH

By Sam Crain ~ "For Karsten with love."

FEY OF THE NIGHT went by many names, but such names were only good for headstones. Survival meant change; no choice about that. Now, they were the so-called Incarnate, those fey who lapped up blood flavored with honey instead of the inverse. Their Seelie foils had done no such rebranding, and look where it got them.

Likewise, regarding branding, Malvina was one of them, the Incarnate. She was an infamous sadomasochist, her name like licking a barbed wire fence. Her specialty was iron, in spite of—because of—the burns and vomiting that metal induced in her kind. When she had nothing better to do, she stole screws and other bits of metal from construction sites, whatever wouldn't be missed but chanced havoc if absconded with. The iron scalded her, but she prided herself on using bare hands, eyes, and face, giggling at the human signs urging face, eye, and hand protection. Contrariety was breath to her; to be was to rebel, and to obey was to cease to exist.

Malvina found him on one of her favorite construction sites, the parking lot of a defunct home goods store. Martyn was a Haunter, so-called; a member of a group of mortals who, in the lead-up and aftermath of Samhain, ran a haunted house attraction that grew like a temporary fungus, its holdings fortified with iron chain-link fencing.

Beyond it, a legend in black-lit neon paint promised 'Screams of Terror.' Simulated blood punctuated the oath, and Malvina chuckled in admiration of the symmetry.

It would be easy. She'd long watched these eager, socially awkward, gleeful mortals, and one particular caught her eye, a blisteringly hot night in October, after sunset. Unseasonable it was, but so was he. He'd stayed later, this one—she read from his brow that he'd gotten there earlier, too. Suffering had writ on his face with a bold hand, lines cutting deep into visible skin, though Malvina's practiced eye saw that the rest of him would be like milk, cool and smooth to touch—almost shaded-marble fine. She licked her lips, aroused by the prospect. His soul was bared to her in the way he winced away from full contact, keeping one hand free as often as he might, the shine of his eyes as he covered over that raw sensitivity to scare the paying customers with meticulously applied gore. He did not shriek like the others, but contorted his frame, lips, and cheeks, presenting himself, a silent grotesque, until the patrons saw those eagerly radiant eyes and screamed or shied away. He smelt of mangos—exotic fruit flavoring cleanser.

He would be her contribution to the Tiend. Thus, she called it still, though her master called it Tithe now, in deference to modernity. The master even shaped 'Halloween' with his forked, deceiving tongue, forsaking the name of Samhain, though he could no more lie than any other of their Folk. They each gave one mortal, not like other courts that made do with a single sacrifice, throat laid open on an altar of cold mirror-bright stone. Call it Hell or the Abyss or What-You-Will, it hungered for flesh. And it meant to savor its offerings in its Great Maze. Their suffering was the Tiend, not their death. It was meant to be long and slow, to begin in pleasure, their torment slaked the Appetite by degrees. Sacrifices either escaped the Maze and had nightmares to further feed the Appetite, or they died within and were digested over time. Both kinds of victims served the purpose, and the Appetite had no preference.

Sure of her quarry, Malvina waited outside the employee entrance of the Haunt. He fed a length of chain through the eleven-gauge fence like a tongue and locked them together. It excited her sexually. It was now or never. Such was a diverting little lie she liked to tell herself—fey being elementally forbidden to lie to others. But self-lies were useful to alleviate the monotony of immortality.

Malvina fondled a fistful of black screws in her pocket and watched on. Martyn, her prey if he but knew it, was in his car, but he'd not yet driven away. He'd locked his wallet into the glove compartment and was checking that he had—three times, four times, seven times all told. Then his seatbelt catch. Seven. Malvina's fey heart ached at the perfection of him.

She walked over and slipped into the passenger seat of his car, intoxicated by the iron that was everywhere in its skeleton. “Thought I’d lost you in the dark, I did,” she said, turning all the glamorous power of her smile on him.

Martyn blinked. “How?” He cleared his throat, sweat visible at his temples, reflecting the yellow streetlight glow. “You came through the Haunt,” he said. “I remember you.”

Her smile widened. “It is good to be memorable,” she agreed. “Give a lady a ride into the woods? We’ve much to celebrate.” He blinked again and half-thought of resisting—she saw his eyelids twitch—but the glamor was strong and underneath his good sense, he was willing. She watched the word register, blooming across his face like a blush: *we*.

••·•·••••·••••

To be lonely and to be alone were not the same thing. Martyn was particularly qualified to know—because he was both. The striking Haunt patron—her hair almost mirror bright, obsidian more than jet—had slipped into his car, into his life like a shoulder into a ball-socket. And he wanted her. It was immediate, inexorable, drowning in her eyes, the sound of her voice, ready to do anything for another glimpse, the barest touch.

"Pull over here." Her breath stirred the hair beside his ear, and his throat constricted as he slid the car into Park. She laughed a little and touched his sweaty arm, bringing all the fine hairs there to attention. Her fingers traveled lower, and he groaned without meaning to, his head suddenly loose on his neck.

"That will do for now," she said, opening her door. Martyn scrambled to follow her on not-quite-steady legs. "Come."

The air smelled of pine and dry leaves—live oak, mainly. A few of their long, narrow acorns glinted in the moonlight. It was a regional park—he'd driven past it hundreds of times but never gone inside. Could he lie down among the acorns and pine needles with this beautiful woman whose name he did not yet know? Such things had never come naturally to him before—

Perhaps things could be different. First time for everything. He didn't have to be such a stick in the mud, for once.

Jenny had come out for college from Back East. She'd always said it like that. Martyn had run into her at St. Vincent de Paul's, where he'd been scoping out prop materials and cheap videotapes. (That's how long ago it had been, and how old he was—though come to think of it, St. Vinnie's still sold videocassettes and they were cheaper than ever, if only he still had a VCR.) Jenny had been hunting for a toaster oven for her dorm room and had noticed his cart of horror tapes and plastic armor pieces. It had started a conversation between them.

She was actually a few years older than he was, despite being a first-year student, because she'd put it off to look after her dad while he had cancer. She didn't tell him this in the middle of the thrift shop—but over dinner the next night. "It's weird, getting set free by somebody dying," she'd said between bites of spinach ravioli he'd refused her offer to try.

Jenny had loved him after a few months. And she'd stayed seven years for him, drawing out her degree as long as possible, moving into an apartment even smaller than his once she finally felt too old and worldly for the dorms. Their living together never quite came up, and Martyn sensed this was more his fault than hers—and was relieved she'd never pressed the matter herself.

But then it had been her mother's turn to start dying, so Jenny had finished her degree at last and returned Back East. She never exactly asked Martyn to go with her, and he didn't offer, but he wasn't an idiot. She'd wanted him to, she'd have said yes. He hadn't been ready or certain enough. So she'd gone back alone, and while they'd kept in touch, it had never been the same. He didn't blame her. But Jenny wasn't the reason for his sevens. He could no longer remember how that had started. Therapists had tried to get him to recall its origin, but it was lost in him somewhere. And he did tend to think of her and those years as he counted in his head because it was such a dazzling coincidence.

"Nearly there," the stranger said, her breath against his neck, and then the slight nip of her teeth. He reached reflexively for her hand, and she closed her fingers around his, drawing him between two trees grown together into a rustic arch. She pulled him close and kissed him, mouth and forehead, before breaking from his hold to enter a maze. He went after, though she was too fleet of foot for him to keep her pace.

Unlike the particleboard maze at Haunt, the dark walls were stone that flickered, giving the impression of dense tree branches, but without any obvious light source. He made directional choices and instinctively braced for jump scares. None came, and his shoes made report against the stone floor—until a *squish* interrupted them. Martyn's erection deflated at the sensation of tepid water filling his socks, but he hesitated only a moment before continuing into a black metal pipe. No telling how it had come to be there, set just a few inches below the floor. He couldn't see where it went. Pitch-dark was no mere figure of speech here, and he put his hands out in his sudden blindness, only to recoil at the sensation of wet hair, gooey with soap scum. Touching it, his nostrils filled with the sickly sweet odors of old shampoo, bar soap, shaving cream—all mingling uneasily with the tangled hair. He swallowed down nausea and tried to feel his way backward, only to find he'd been sealed in like a letter in an envelope. The hair-scum forest had sprouted behind as well as before.

No way out but through.

Martyn shook. He prayed to a god he didn't believe in to get him out of there, to wake him up. It was a nightmare—the worst tactile hallucination of his life. Worse than anything that the weasels, those harbingers of thoughts he had without his own consent, had ever forced him to imagine. His eyes were propped open against his will, like that fellow in *A Clockwork Orange*.

No way out but through.

He'd have to feel his way, every step, every inch. No other choice, no Option C. Gagging a little, tasting salt tears on his tongue, he half-fell forward, and it evoked swimming, digging, even tearing—without being truly like any of those things.

It would be easier to breathe at the bottom of a swimming pool, he thought over the pounding of his errant heart.

Martyn was tiring, and yet there was more slimy hair to work through. He'd thought his pulse would simply quicken til he collapsed and died, strangled on the queen mother of all hairballs—but his heart found an equilibrium instead, faster than healthy but livable, barely.

And then he was out into the next part of the maze. Smooth marble flags were under his feet again as though he were in the corridor of a grand edifice, perhaps a cathedral. He was barefoot—little wonder he'd lost his shoes in that mess back there. The cool stone on the soles of his feet was downright pleasant after the squish of the drainpipe. He braced his hands on his knees, getting his breath back. With his heart rate stable again, he walked on.

A blast of air nearly knocked him to the stone, but there were other blasts too—sounds glancing off his ribs like snares, kickdrums, cymbals, and a siren. He was sandwiched between the rushing air and the shocking sounds, the colored lights searing against his retinas: pus-yellow, the maroon of slow-drying blood, snot green. He remembered the robot at the end of the Haunt Maze.

They should have saved this for the final scare, he thought. Amateurs, to spend it all in only the second room. He was not naïve enough to think this was all the maze had to throw at him. But surely, you saved the full-on panic attack for the finale—

The jump scare, or whatever it was, drained Martyn of his strength to escape it. A corridor opened up a few meters away, but he couldn't stop the scare. It broke upon him like a beach wave. All he could do was to force himself to keep breathing. In. Out. Jenny would be so proud. She'd believed in him, once.

The Threshold was a sensation as much as the physical appearance of a landmark, a swoop of his stomach as he stubbed his bare toes against the base support of a ladder that had not been there before. The first rung, though, was nearly at his neck. His heart thundered, but the rest of the noise had abated, for now.

Climb up. The ladder's demand could not have been clearer, rickety or not. *How many other hands have clung to these rungs?* Martyn wondered, scrubbing his futilely on the tatters of his clothes, as if it could dry them or clean them. *Five, six, seven.*

Seeing a decorously severed head, its eyes covered in a black cloth blindfold hanging from a fine silver chain, his heart went cold. He thought: *their installations are improving.* Perhaps even magical beings got better with practice, for it was surely magic. It didn't follow reason that there should be a torture-maze perfectly tailored to his fears—his compulsions. It was as though the weasels, his worst fear, had dreamed this place out of whole cloth and clipped the stray threads with their worrying teeth.

He pulled himself up onto the ladder and counted the rungs in sevens too, until he lost count. When he was halfway, a cadence echoed through the empty space behind the ladder, a recognizable heartbeat—not simply human but belonging to one he had lost. The recognition was a knife to the chest.

The sevens did not come from Jenny. He knew that. They were something else—and he *did* know, here and now: the number of times Daddy had left him for the 'emergency.' That seventh time, almost-eight-year-old Marty had figured out Mommy was what grown-ups called *on a drunk,* and Daddy had to pick up the pieces while Marty waited, hearing the living room clock tick.

He'd forgotten this, until now, breathing in the reek of stale beer and spilt whiskey. *This* was why he'd instinctively avoided bars, the reason for his aversion to alcohol. Mommy had gotten sober—quick enough for that whole episode to be forgotten. She hadn't abused him, stayed married to Daddy. It was a blip that marked him. Was that funny? Even the babysitter had been all right, Martyn remembered, getting a grip on himself with a claustrophobic effort. She'd made him popcorn on the stovetop and tucked him into bed on time, all perfectly above board. It was almost anticlimactic that his original seven didn't start from a grand trauma.

He was well above the floor of this not-quite-cathedral, and nowhere near the top of the ladder. He couldn't see the ceiling, either, even when he craned his neck.

Screams bounced off his ribcage like physical blows, and those *were* Jenny, somehow. "Oh, God, Jenny," he murmured deep in his throat. *Imagine a Haunt device that could replicate a loved one's voice in anguish. Some kind of AI generator?* he thought. Except using such a thing, even if it did exist, would make him an actual monster rather than a pretend one. He climbed on and thought of her, thought of her and counted sevens, trying to avoid the teeth.

Teeth.

His were sharp. He'd crossed over another Threshold, it seemed, and now his teeth were pointed, and he had fur prickling over his whole body. Off the ladder, he walked on all fours. The long, bald tail that twitched behind him came as a relief—he'd feared for a wild moment that he'd become a weasel after spending four-fifths of his life trying to propitiate the ones that made shameless dens in his mind and gnashed their incisors at him whenever he resisted their arbitrary demands, those boundary lines that made sense to no one, not least Martyn himself. Better to be even a rat than a weasel.

The wave of scent hit him as intensely as a body blow: piss, shit, and greasy sludge worse than the hair-scum had been. He hoisted himself up onto a fine mesh grating, which barely covered the sewage below. The liquid splashed up in places, and Martyn choked on the smell. A rat might be hardier than a man, but its nose was also more acute, and his twitched convulsively with the stench of it all as he ran. His paws were long since coated in the heinous admixture, and he was nauseated almost beyond bearing.

Run: a simple imperative, but not easily honored as he wobbled on half-familiar paws, scraping them on the grating. He'd give his soul to wash them clean.

The urge to vomit was intolerable, the weasels whispering that he should not, while Jenny would have said it'd make him feel better. Despite this, he pushed onward, the nausea building as a sharp crescendo of sensation in the underbelly of his mind, and yet, in a stomach chamber of that same mind was a single ripe, golden image that startled the darkness into fragments:

Cheese.

Martyn's blood ran colder than ever. Here, now, a rat-ly thought, rather than a human one. He was running himself ragged, and all at once, he froze, trembling throughout his be-furred frame. He looked down, gasping, and saw his blood dripping through the grating into the sewage that churned below—

Then, he added his vomit to the mix, copiously and with violence, covering himself with it before it trickled down through the slotted walkway. It lasted a long while—a day, for all he knew—and then he could breathe again, counting the scents in his mind. Of course there were seven: piss, shit, grease, sweat, tears, blood, and, finally, *vomitus.*

There, a chink of light revealed a way out. He ran on bloodied pads, not thinking of anything but freedom. He felt himself pass over the Threshold and was once again on two legs and of his ordinary size. The transformation had claimed what was left of his clothes.

Martyn found himself in a room of polished stone with carved rafters. The ceiling was crystal, and the night sky was visible through it—the pre-dawn sky, he amended himself, for it was grey-edged in fine, bright silver, if the sky could still be trusted.

She was there. She reclined on a seat draped in cerulean silk, holding a crystal goblet of pale green wine. A second glass sat on a tray by her elbow, and she toasted him. He drew near her, uncertain but unable to withstand his powerful attraction to her, which he could not hope to conceal at all without clothes. "Your name?" he asked, his voice all breath.

She laughed with a full throat. "We do not part with those cheaply as mortals do, Martyn Reginald Cooper. But think of me as Malvina, if you will. It serves as well as any." She offered her own goblet like a challenge.

Malvina, he thought, and took a shallow sip of the green wine. It tasted like sunshine and wind, and he suspected that in accepting her hospitality he had made a mistake, but he swallowed once.

"Such a fertile imagination for torment. I scarcely need dirty a finger." Malvina licked his finger, sucked it like a marrow bone, and he nearly gave in. He wavered on a knife's edge until Malvina tore open her own finger and wrote on his forehead and lips with the welling blood. He could taste something wholly without referent in his mouth. Alcohol for magical beings.

"Stay a time, won't you? There's so much left to see." Only, he didn't writhe or shrink—and he didn't abandon himself to her, either. He was ready to run now. The sky peeked out beyond this vestibule or atrium or whatever it was, and he would trust that sky, if nothing else. Malvina was only one of the weasels in the end, for all her beauty. He need not obey her whims at his own expense, no matter what she did to his body.

He escaped the strange room. Tree branches knocked against his face as he crossed the final Threshold, and he could breathe soft night air, feeling it a little cold against his bloody face. He could just about remember where his car was, and he had his costume duster in the trunk. If he made it back there, he could drive home without getting arrested.

He thought of that duster, weakening at its seams but still serviceable, as he ran over pine needles, dead leaves, pebbles, and those pointy damned acorns. For a wonder, he kept his balance. He would likely be picking things out of his feet for days, but he was alive and freer than he'd ever felt. He would shower when he got home because he was actually filthy, not because the weasels whispered about not knowing where the bugs had been as they landed next to him.

Real filth felt almost aspirational against his skin as his car edged into view.

Honest filth.

SOUL FOOD

By Matthew Christian

WHEN I WOKE UP, I was no longer human. I shifted my six crooked legs, but they failed to lift the feathered bulk of my body and wriggled like snakes in the grass. The joints were weak—soft and wrong like rubber bands soaked in anesthetic.

I struggled to look from my useless appendages to a bird flying overhead, then saw another animal nearby, fat and feathered like me. It stood in the sunny pasture on five stilt-like legs. Behind it, a rectangle had been cut out of the picturesque scene, leaving a black void.

I pushed again, the numbness loosening from my joints like ice thawing in the spring. A hoof connected with the ground and held a modicum of weight. Another found footing, then another. The middle leg on my left side jangled awkwardly as I struggled up, the pin-pricking lameness refusing to give me control. I knew that if I could just get the other legs under me, I'd be stable.

The last of the hooves slid around, found their grip, and I shakily stood like a newborn calf. The feathers along my belly were bent at odd angles. A gray and white smattering of them lay abandoned in the grass.

I drew air through the nostrils that pockmarked my beak as the others circled. I could only watch as their feathers of white, brown, and soft blue closed in. Drawn forward on varying numbers of legs—three, four, some five—their missing leg joints swelled with scar tissue.

They regarded me with wide-eyed interest. Had there never been a six-legged animal like me before—is that why they stared in apparent fear?

One of them hobbled forward on two legs, a funhouse mirror version of my own shape. I only realized the great size of these animals as he approached, towering on legs of engorged muscle like a nightmare Clydesdale. A crack ran along his beak where shattered slivers of keratin hung on scabbed flesh. The pieces rose and fell with each breath.

In one quick motion, he unfurled four wings, his feathers stretched out in a ragged display of aggression. Though it was clear his wings were stubs of what they once were, ending at knobs of scar tissue sprayed chalky orange, he was majestic and terrifying.

Without warning, he jabbed at me, gouging the flesh above my eye with his sawtooth beak. Blood popped from the wound and splashed across the grass, then trickled into my eye.

He let out a wretched caw. Even without words, I got the message—this was his territory. Satisfied, he closed his wings and backed away with the dissipating herd, leaving me alone.

I cowered in fear, wondering how the hell I had gotten here—how I had become this thing. Images of the night before ran through my mind: the boys fighting over the last slice of pizza, Marshall snatching it away from his younger brother and running his tongue over the crust and Garrett's loud "*yuck*" as he left the table; Leah and I lying in bed, a space between us—too much space; falling asleep in the pages of a book on couples' communication.

I would give anything to hear her now, to give her the '*I love you*' she never got that night.

This had to be a nightmare, a gross trick my brain played on me while I slept—after all, these animals weren't real. Not that I knew of, anyway. I would wake up, kiss Leah, and make the boys pancakes. But blood still trickled down my face, and Shatterbeak's attack had hurt too much to be anything less than real.

I stretched, the muscles in my back tightening until my wings unfurled and flopped against the floor. Over and over, I pulled at them, surprised by their weight, and my eyes caught the flash of paint at their snipped ends. The missing ends buzzed inside my mind like ghostly whispers from phantom feathers.

A sliver of light split the void rectangle and grew, two panels sliding open to reveal an audience of overweight humans. Their beady eyes glared at us, their wide smiles pushing up their chubby cheeks. They spoke excitedly, but no sound came through the window. They hovered in metal carriers snugged around their rotund bodies, and beneath them hung withered, rotten legs, blackened and dead.

The children, whose legs were only beginning to decay, rode in brightly colored carriers stamped with cartoon characters. They wore floppy caps with plastic horns and dumped neon-colored liquid into their mouths. The awed gaze of the adults made me feel rare and powerful, like a firework. The kids' lack of interest, however, made me feel as common and unwanted as a penny kicked into a sewer.

Help me, I screamed, *for God's sakes, help me!* But all that came out was a strained bugle sound that reminded me of elk hunting with my brother-in-law.

A chime jangled in the meadow air, followed by a booming voice. "When J. P. Doonan was born into a family of cattle ranchers, no one suspected just how influential he'd become to the future of bioengineering. Who knew the youngest of four would one day lead scientists to create sustainable, environmentally conscious, and most importantly, *delicious* animal products? Our award-winning chiquine are a viral sensation not simply because of their looks, but for their innovative taste."

"J.P.'s secret is in his recipe," the voice continued, laying into the heavy southern accent. "A recipe he locked away in an airtight vault only he and his brother have access to. Though J.P. passed away in 4588, his tradition for fresh-cut chiquine steaks continues here at J.P.'s Family Farmhouse—where our farmhouse is your family."

I ran, putting as much distance as possible between me and the window. Green hills sprawled out ahead of me, and I galloped away from the chiquine herd. I would run and never look back, never return to Shatterbeak's meadow or the window.

I crashed into something only yards from where I started, as if the hand of God himself swatted me across the beak. I dropped, stunned, the field swimming in my vision. The open plains ahead flickered, disappearing and reappearing in flashes of existence.

It was a wall... no, a screen. There was no sky, no birds, and no fields; it was all fake. That was why the others huddled together so tightly. We were in a cell on display—on the menu.

Another chime from the speakers. "Please form a single-file queue behind the yellow line. Our attendant will take your order promptly. Be sure to ask about our family-sized discounts on leg and wing combo meals."

I paced in horror as the first family hovered forward to an attendant in an old-timey periwinkle dress and curled hair. A boy searched our herd, eyeing each chiquine. Then, his eyes held me in their hungry gaze. He thump, thump, thumped his little finger on the glass. Standing along the back of the cell, thick walls of metal and plastic separating us, I could still read his lips.

That one.

His parents looked at me with sick greed while the attendant tapped on a tablet. I felt the thrum of a chip vibrate beneath the skin above my mid-left haunch. The boy and his family faded into the dark, replaced by hungrier eyes.

The seemingly unending line of customers continued to pick their chiquine. I watched the herd anxiously move about—my God, they understood what was happening. The other chiquine were more like me than I realized, more *human.*

Seventeen customers, many of them families, spoke to the attendant. All seventeen groups had lingered on me at some point while choosing - five more buzzing chips in me by the end, one for each limb.

The last customer, their large body covered in a thick jacket, approached the distracted attendant while she finalized the previous order. Suddenly, the jacket opened, and legs, muscular and rigid, unfurled from within, the carrier and its attached fake legs swinging away. He gripped a pipe-like object and swung at her, producing a sickening crack that echoed through the barrier and splattered its surface in bright patterns of blood.

The hooded figure hastily swiped a can through the air, painting words across the window: *DEFY SOUL FOOD—DEFY J.P.'S!!*

He took the pipe and struck the fortified glass, the *clunk* ringing in the cell. The herd rushed around me, madly circling. I had no choice but to follow them, afraid with every step that my lame leg would trip me. Another *clunk* and a web of cracks appeared beside the yellow words. My heart pounded in my chest as we sped up, but my chiquine body relished in the new pace—a pace that would have burned the lungs of my human body. The cool air I sucked in with each stride filled me with energy, driving me on.

Something thumped beneath my hooves, threatening to bring me down—but my legs clambered over it. Blood stung my eye from the cut on my head, and I shook to clear it. We circled the room, the obstacle banging against my shins again and again.

Several laps later, I realized the obstacle was a body—the blood in my eyes not from my wound but spray from the chiquine we feverishly trampled. I wanted to stop, but the herd moved autonomously, mindlessly. With each pass, my feet ground the battered remains of Shatterbeak into the concrete floor.

It was then that the pipe broke through. With each pass, the hole grew—the pipe appearing like a groundhog peeking from its hole. In the light of the window, I saw the customers rush and tackle the hooded figure, the weight of their carriers driving him against the far wall. The wailing sounds of the fight slipped in through the opening, complementing the chaotic drumming of our crazed galloping.

I tracked the breach in the glass as I ran. The hole—now about the size of a car tire—filled me with a courage I had lacked since waking up. We were no longer separated from the world. The door was open; there was an escape. All I needed to do was go through.

Finding a break from the herd, I pressed into a corner away from the blind rush. I tightly circled the spot to gather traction, then charged through the herd. With every muscle I could gather, I leapt into the air, crashing headfirst through the breach—the window shattering against the weight of my body.

I landed inside the dark room where hungry customers stared in horror. Shocked by making it through the window, I stared back. The body of the hooded figure lay discarded to my left, silent and unmoving.

Sharp pain emanated from my lame leg where it had dragged across the window shards. I looked back to find the feathers there growing dark with blood. In the cascading light of the menu overhead, a ragged piece of reinforced glass lingered in the frame, the window smiling with the bloody teeth that bit me.

Another attendant waved her arms at me as if that would scare me back into the cell. I would *never* go back there. I charged, racing headfirst past her and into the group. Customers whizzed their hover seats out of the way; others sped out the door I ran toward.

I raced out of the ordering room and down a hallway. Clopping hooves echoed on the floor behind me as the herd followed. I passed dozens of ordering room doors in a blur, the walls between them lined with screens playing promotional videos, looping J.P.'s evolution from a roadside stand beside the Oklahoman highway to an internationally franchised chain.

My hooves screeched to a clumsy stop on the slick floor, and I huffed to catch my breath. I found myself in a warehouse-sized dining room with multiple floors and hundreds of overweight humans gathered around endless rows of tables.

I searched for an exit through unsteady eyes—the world ticking back and forth in my vision. The glass had nicked something in me that wouldn't stop leaking. The once minor blood spot on my hind now engulfed the rest of the leg, and a red trail traced my path back through the hall.

The herd dashed wildly past me, crashing through the room like a tidal wave. Tables toppled, plates shattered, and chiquine steaks spun across the floor. The hoverchairs couldn't move the customers' engorged bodies fast enough—the chiquine were mad with freedom, blindly trampling anything and anyone in their way. It took seconds for the herd to destroy the room, breaking through an exit at the far end before disappearing.

I followed, but only made it midway through the room before my body—sluggish and woozy—forced me to slow down. My hooves clacked against the lacquered floor, echoing in the room where those who still clung to life cried out for help. They looked up at me, the hunger in their eyes replaced with fear.

At the exit, automatic doors lay ripped from their tracks, twitching as the gears tried to tug them back. There was no going back, or was there? J.P.'s would fix the door, clean up the blood, and dispose of the bodies. J.P.'s would reopen, and we would be back on the menu.

Outside the door, the world bobbed, floating in a vast ocean of neon. Screens covered the sides of rundown skyscrapers that disappeared high above in a sickly brown smog. Chub-faced residents peeked out of the tightly packed windows or hovered on small balconies. Their outlines were lit by the ads on the screens, some featuring fresh-cut chiquine steaks.

Car horns blared from a street ahead where the herd had run through. In the distance, the wail of sirens and gunshots penetrated the hum of the city. People hovered in alleys and against buildings, waiting to see if there were more of us.

My legs shook, knees turning to rubber. I extended my wings as far as I could, feeling the breeze flutter through my feathers and hair. The cool air reminded me of summer nights on the farm as autumn crept in. I closed my eyes, replaying the memories of those nights when Leah and I drank sweet tea, the boys played in the fields, and we'd soaked up the last rays of summer sun. Then I opened my eyes, and it was all gone—my family, the sun, my life.

The gunshot echoed in the valley of the screens, the dart piercing my shoulder. In seconds, the spinning world turned black.

•••••••••••

I was flying. I kicked the daze from my limbs, trying my best to scrape the coated flooring but never quite reaching it. My legs spilled from holes in a canvas reinforced with chains that ran to the ceiling. The room was clinically white except for more chiquine held in similar hoists.

A newly lamed leg dangled below where the dart had hit me. I knew this feeling; it was the same lameness my other leg had had, and I finally understood—they drugged me to get me into the cell before I gained consciousness. That's why the leg had never recovered feeling.

To my horror, the hind leg on the other side, which had been the source of my bleeding, was missing. A cauterized wound marred my hip. I'd become food.

Two men lingered beside me, one young and lanky on two legs, the old one slouched in a carrier, both wearing coverings that left only their faces visible. The young one, barely past his teens, stared at me while the other swiped on a tablet, his leatherlike skin accentuating the wrinkles stretching across his forehead.

"You take care'uh the next one," the old man said, never looking up from the tablet.

"But, it's- it's awake," the boy stammered. "What if it *feels* it?"

"They don't pay us enough to give a good damn what *it* feels. Orders in, meat out, an' if you ain't fast enough, they'll get rid of you. Ain't enough time for me to care."

"They say it's souls, you know. They make 'em with dead souls to taste better."

"You one'uh them soul food activist *assholes*?" His eyes glared at the legs the boy stood on. "They're why we got that mandatory time off. They're why we didn't get paid again until yesterday."

"No, sorry," the boy said. "It's just... scary. What if they use me after I die?"

"Ain't worth worrying about what you don't know. That's why they call it a *secret* recipe. All's I know is chiquine come in on the truck sleepin' like a baby, and when they're picked, I get to cuttin'."

The boy stayed silent. In the closeness between us, I saw the fear in his eyes. In that moment, I wasn't sure who was worse off, the chiquine or the humans.

"Alright now," the old man continued, "you're cuttin' R3. Corporate wants all employees to try the new dry rub—guess so we can tell customers it ain't shit when they ask."

He pulled a metal rod from the side of his cart and handed it to the boy. The boy looked at him and hesitated, then walked toward my left side.

"Other side, *R3*!"

The boy hurried to my right and turned the rod on. A beam sputtered along its side, buzzing like a hummingbird. He gripped one of my legs, and at the touch, I kicked, my hoof connecting with his leg and sending him stumbling backwards.

The old man laughed. "She givin' you hell, eh, boy?"

The boy gathered himself, then returned with anger in place of his fear. He pressed the beam against my skin, and I howled in pain as he got to cutting.

•••••••••••••

I've lost count of the days. I would count them when the employees closed for the night, but I've since stopped. My body is aging; so is my mind.

They've eaten my legs, those hungry people who picked me. Of my six legs, only one good one remains, and one lame. I've learned to prop the lame leg beneath me—a fleshy cane that helps me shuffle. It's rotted and shrunk over time, and when the window opens, they see it and quickly move on.

Like Shatterbeak, I've become the last of the old batch, so the other chiquine leave me alone. Every day, new chiquine appear—the eyes always find them first. Most of them rarely last a day, a couple of days tops.

I used to bark and screech when they'd appear, begging for them to pick me, but they never do. Had I not broken out of the room and scarred up my leg, I would have been fully consumed. So, now I spend my days lying in a fake meadow, watching digital birds fly past, knowing death would have been the better end.

THE TOWER

By Elana Gomel

SHE MOVES SLOWLY ACROSS the room, her fingers groping in the thick darkness like the tentacles of a sea anemone, tasting the dead air. She collides with something—a side table, a stool?—and it clatters upon the invisible floor with an obscene rattle echoed in the depths of the building.

Outside the floor-to-ceiling window, the white sky is glowing with afternoon heat. Not a scintilla of light penetrates the room. She can see the day outside, so bright it hurts her eyes to look. But inside the apartment is occupied by night. The boundary between light and darkness is as sharp as a razor blade, shredding time.

••·•·••·•··•·••

Bodies found.

NextDoor was exploding with indignation. They were building a high-rise in our town.

High-rise? I snorted and closed the app. The new housing development, next to my rented townhouse, was a paltry four-story block with studios and two-bedroom apartments meant to entice young techies into paying exorbitant prices for faux city living. It was not a high-rise. It was not in the city. And sure as hell, it was not affordable.

Now, this alarmist post about "bodies" uncovered in the excavation, quickly taken down by the moderators. I could not understand people's hostility to the idea of tall buildings. I always dreamed of stone-and-glass towers, challenging the sky. I wished I could live on the hundredth floor of some stupendous construction floating far above the suburban sprawl. But there were no skyscrapers in the Bay Area. My friends who had traveled to Europe and Asia described the Shard in London and the Burj Khalifa in Dubai, but I had never been outside the US, at least not in my adult life. I was still hungry after my healthy breakfast of fruit and coffee, but I forbade myself from even thinking of food. I started putting on weight, and I hated it. Before getting into my beat-up Honda Civic, a dark smear insinuated itself into my field of vision, overlaying my reflection in the mirror with a shadow that bisected my face. But there was nothing there to cast it.

I took out the contact lens, rinsed it, and put it back in. No shadows. No smears. No stray bits of mascara. Just the soulless flat light that evened out my complexion into a pancake-like blob of generic foundation and appropriately understated blush. As always, I had that tiny hitch of non-recognition my face provoked.

Stuck in bumper-to-bumper traffic, the Honda crawled by the hastily erected fencing around the excavation for the new development. In the gaps between the slats, I glimpsed the hole, yawning like a raw wound left from a removed tooth.

My mother's face blinked on the phone screen. I sighed and accepted the call.

"Jinnie?" she asked. When talking to me, my mother always sounded apprehensive, as if the unspoken weight of everything she had done wrong or thought she had done wrong in her parenting was teetering behind her words, threatening to crash down and bury both of us.

"Yes, Mum?"

"How's it going? Are you OK? Do you need money?"

The car in front of me changed lanes, and I pushed into the minuscule space. Somebody honked. The Bay Area traffic, formerly genteel and polite, was unraveling as the roads were clogged with motorcycles, EVs, and assorted hybrids.

"Mum, I am making a decent salary. I don't need your money!"

In truth, I might need it soon. After our breakup, Cory moved out, and I had to pay the exorbitant rent out of my own pocket. But I was reluctant to ask her. My mother's sense of guilt was transferring to me through the osmosis of our claustrophobic relationship.

"But Jinnie..."

"My name is Jennifer, Mum," I said.

It was not. I did not know what my name was.

••·•·••●··•·••

She is hungry. She does not remember when she last ate. The darkness devours time, and the quick flutter of day and night outside blends into the meaningless background of being here, inside the tower. But there is a weight in her belly, something pressing upon her diaphragm, squashing her innards and making it hard to breathe.

She plummets into the depths of herself, searching.

•••••••••••••

The bottle was a pricy Viognier. When Cory still lived with me, neither of us would have thought of drinking alone. I hesitated before pouring. My period was a couple of days late, and a feathery doubt tickled the back of my mind. But whatever happened, I was not going to have kids, so...

I sipped the wine and sat down to watch a South Korean zombie movie.

Mr. Skittles leaped onto my lap, his upright tail tickling my face. I brushed it aside. It subsided but left a visual trace like the contrail of a jet: a vertical shadow. I blinked, but it did not go away.

On the screen, a warren of small rooms, stitched together by an Esher-like maze of stairs, was overrun by garishly made-up undead. Characters were yelling, their incomprehensible sibilance of terror splashing onto my TV in lines of subtitles. The camera zoomed out, showing a group of skyscrapers like a cluster of crystals under the inflamed sky.

One of the skyscrapers detached itself from the screen and floated in the air before me: an image becoming part of my living room's reality. It was like a little girl crawling out of the TV in a Japanese movie whose name I forgot. I jumped, dislodging Mr. Skittles from my lap, who hissed indignantly.

I downed the Viognier in one gulp and made an appointment with an ophthalmologist.

••·•·••••·•·••

She lies down on the hardwood floor. The darkness embraces her with its shapeless, velvety arms. She is sinking into it, feeling her boundaries dissolve and flow, the weight inside her spreading out like a blot, consuming her.

There is a faint clacking sound coming from somewhere. Like castanets, she thinks dreamily.

Like bones.

•• · • · • · • · • · • · • ••

The doctor was new, and I had to fill in one of those intrusive insurance forms. I did not even pause over the list of racial categories, marking "Asian American" with practiced ease. When I was a child, Mum had filled out these forms for me, and I still remember the last time I looked over her shoulder and saw her hand hesitate over "Caucasian."

Of course, I had always known I was adopted. It was impossible to overlook the contrast between my mother's midwestern face and my own features. In the exurb of Des Moines where I grew up, the sight of the two of us occasionally caused a flicker of unease, a veiled glance that settled on my skin like a hairy moth. I supposed the presence of my blond and burly adoptive father would have made it even worse, but he had left when I was five and had not been in touch since. I felt better being in California on my own. Though Chinese adoptions were recently discontinued, there were plenty of Asians around.

The doctor examined my eyes with spooky-looking machinery and made notations on my chart.

"Everything seems all right," she said reluctantly, as if my absence of impairment was a personal affront. "Though... there seems to be some clouding of the retina, very minor, but still unusual in such a young person. Do you have any history of macular degeneration in your family, Ms. Hartcliff?"

"I wouldn't know," I said.

•• · • · • · • · • · • · • · ••

She is hungry again. She gets up and bumps into a sharp corner. She can see perfectly well into the sky beyond the glass wall. Gaps in the white pall of clouds or pollution, like the sun is burning through its cottony padding, reveal pale glimpses of fleeing blue. A bird passes across the expanse of light, a curlicue of blackness like an unreadable message. But the darkness inside the room is implacable, as heavy as stagnant water.

•••••••••••••

The shadow in my eye did not go away. It came back again and again, first alarming, then annoying, then expected, just a part of daily routine, much like traffic jams and Cory's occasional accusatory text. And it soon became more than a shadow. It solidified into a three-dimensional image—a tower.

Not like the castle towers in the soggy adaptations of Tolkien or those stupid fantasy games Cory liked so much. Not a pseudo-medieval construction adorned with useless battlements. It was a steel-and-concrete spire, tall enough to pierce the sky, dotted with the unblinking eyes of innumerable windows. It had a jutting steeple shaped like the eye of a needle. It was steely gray and corpse blue.

A skyscraper, one of those architectural ziggurats that dot China's enormous cities—Shenzhen, Shanghai, Chongqing—rising 2000, 1700, and 1500 feet.

I spent my free time trawling architectural websites and forums. The tallest building in the world was not in China anymore; it was the Burj Khalifa in Dubai. But I was convinced that the tower overlaying itself on the meaningless bustle of my existence was in China. It was not a hallucination. It was a memory. My history was returning, giving me back the stolen time before the childless couple in Iowa whisked me away to live out their tattered American Dream.

Nobody has memories of their babyhood. Your name is Jennifer. Your mother lives in Iowa.

Lies, all lies.

I started posting pictures of Chinese skyscrapers on my feeds with hashtags like #wishiwasthere. I was seriously considering resigning from my job and traveling to my birthplace. There were two problems. I didn't have enough money to pay rent, let alone travel internationally. And even if I did, I wouldn't know where to go because my mother never told me where she adopted me. I could, of course, sell my Honda, but the idea of being without a car filled me with the same visceral horror as the idea of losing a limb. So, I counted on the economy improving and my company doing better. And meanwhile, I could at least try to solve the second problem.

I swiped through the thicket of notifications to video-call my mother. I had stopped following the fake story about the bodies supposedly found at the site of the new housing development. But now it seemed there was something to it, after all.

"Mum, where was the orphanage you got me from?"

Her face fell. Literally. A waterfall of brightness washed over the tiny screen, and when it faded, my mother's close-up wrinkles had disappeared. For a moment, I seemed to look at the younger version of her. And then it was gone too. Instead, starkly outlined against the blazing sky was the tower—the skyscraper. What had been a shadow on my retina, an elusive image in my dreams, a fluid memory, was now an actual picture.

It was as huge as I always imagined, the picture showing the asphalt of its foundation and a tiny tree dwarfed by its immensity. The skyscraper seemed to be stuck in the middle of an empty plaza, but as I swiped with trembling fingers, trying to expand the picture, I saw other architecture clustering around it like the undergrowth around a redwood tree: malls, apartment blocks, loops of bridges. Gleamingly clean, pristine, and empty. Not a single car on the bridge, not a single pedestrian in the street, not a single flicker of motion anywhere. The timeless beauty of technological sterility.

I stroked it as if my phone were a magic portal that would expand and let me into my world. Instead, the picture washed away in the rain of brightness, and my mother reappeared.

"What's wrong, Jinnie?" she asked, a tear crawling slowly down her cheeks. "You just... you just froze."

"The orphanage, Mum?"

"It was in Guangxi," she said, and ended the video call, which she had never done before.

I stared at the phone's Home screen. More notifications. Yes, bodies were found at the site of the new construction. Old bodies. Bones.

●•·●·•·●•·•●·•●

She finally realizes what the darkness is.

It is her. She is inside her own womb, where a new life grows, a new life to make up for those who had been taken. She is inside and outside, twisted into an impossible loop, a pretzel of spacetime where the past and the future are tied in a Gordian knot. She feebly claws at the strands of herself, trying to unravel them and to find what nestles in the middle.

She is hungry. The building sucks life out of her and pours it into the darkness, into the clutter of furniture, into its concrete and rebar. The building drinks her life force, giving it back to her in a uterine loop.

And still, the hunger is unbearable. A dull ache, an unrelenting pressure, flaring up and subsiding but never leaving her. Hunger is her only companion.

She stumbles across a home altar and slaps her hands on the floor. Perhaps there would be an offering here: an orange, a bottle of water.

Nothing.

She drags herself to the window and beats on the glass, which repels her efforts with the insouciance of architectural hubris. Very far below, streetlights turn on. Nothing moves in their spots of brightness.

But there is movement behind her, in the dark—a clatter.

••·•·••••·••·•••

Cory called. I blocked him. I reminded myself I needed a pregnancy test. We had used birth control, of course, but still... and then I forgot about my fears of being pregnant.

I was too busy sitting at the dinner table in my apartment and doing research.

Ghost cities of China. There are at least fifty of them. Perfectly designed, each a machine for living, as Le Corbusier, a famous Modernist architect, would call them (by this time, I was so deep into architectural websites, books, and blogs that I could recite the difference between modernist and postmodernist urban design in my sleep). I spent hours gazing at those eerie cityscapes, glossy and gleaming, no trash or graffiti, the immaculate sidewalks, glass and chrome, the future of yesterday. And not a single car or pedestrian. Empty, empty, empty.

These cities were built to house the burgeoning population, one that collapsed, to support the expanding economy, one that contracted. Despite my job as a CFO, I was not interested in the economic squabbles that doomed those cities to their immaculate solitude. Instead, I was obsessed with their sheer perfection. I imagined myself walking down those deserted sidewalks and entering the echoing lobbies.

And in one of those skyscrapers, I would find my mother. I did not know how I knew it, but I did.

I requested my original birth certificate.

The process is complicated and tangled in red tape. I needed to apply to the court to get it. But I was adept at dealing with California's bloated bureaucracy. And finally, I held it in my hands.

It meant nothing.

Of course, it didn't. It was in Mandarin. And I could not read a single graceful ideogram that always reminded me of rippling water reflections. My mother hadn't thought it was important for me to learn Chinese. She didn't search for bilingual schools, tutors, or even buy language-learning software.

As I was pondering whether to run the certificate through a translation program or text one of my coworkers who was originally from Shenzhen, an alert blinked on my phone.

The count of bodies found at the construction site rises.

I swiped on it.

On the video feed, police cruisers were clustered around the fenced-off construction site like flies on a roadkill.

Ten bodies? Really?

They were old bodies, the post read. Skeletons. At least seventy years old, if not more. That was reassuring: at least, no new serial killer popped up in California.

I turned off the phone and reached for the birth certificate, determined not to procrastinate anymore. Still, I could not help glancing outside from my apartment's window. I saw the fencing. I saw a police cruiser.

And I saw a tower of steel and glass above it all, looming into the flat American sky.

•••••••••••••

She squats in the corner and feels a warm rush of liquid down her pant leg. She had not eaten or drunk. She had not used the bathroom. In the limbo of darkness and light, bodily functions have been suspended. Only the thing growing inside her defies the time-loop, forcing it back into a linear progression of history: conception, gestation, birth.

It's birth time. Her water has broken.

She hopes the labor pain will still the hunger gnawing at her, but it doesn't. Hunger is inside and outside. Hunger is her.

Her baby is being born—a hunger baby.

A smooth, hard hand pats her face, forcing her to lie down. Her body ripples with contractions.

A dry whisper floats in the dark. It sounds like a name. Ji...

It sounds familiar.

She turns her face to the window. Outside, daylight fades, the white sky turning tender pink and then blooming with red and orange in a brief burst of color that scorches her retinas. And then it dissipates. The sky darkens. Not that it makes any difference. Day and night cycles are for outside. It is always dark inside the tower, just as it is always dark inside her.

"Ji," her dead midwife whispers again.

"What does it mean?" she asks in English, the only language she knows.

"Ji."

•• · • · •• • •• · • · ••

It rose from behind the low roofs of townhouses, dwarfing the suburban sprawl outside my window, turning the sycamore trees planted along my street into grasses around the mighty trunk of a redwood. It was enormous. It was majestic. It was ugly.

Its raw concrete façade was studded with innumerable rows of identical square windows, making me dizzy trying to imagine all those lives squeezed into the tiny rooms. The sheer weight of humanity woven with rebar, steel, and stone was threatening to topple over and squash me like a bug. The tower seemed to expand and contract as if it were breathing, as if it was about to start walking across the sunny street, smashing cars and trampling pedestrians, tearing reality like a flimsy paper screen.

It was here. And it did not exist. There was no high-rise anywhere near my townhouse. There was no high-rise like this anywhere in California.

The body count rises.

Dazed, I lifted my phone to catch up on the news about the construction site and watched the florid face of some local official mouthing platitudes. And then the video feed blinked, and what appeared to be drone footage showed instead. The drone rose above the fenced-in site to reveal a hole in the broken pavement. And lying in it were bones.

More bones than I could imagine: skulls, pelvises, femurs, and joints, all piled up like driftwood, almost beautiful in their abandon, clean and polished by time. They lay in that hole like the foundations of beams or supports ready for construction, and for a moment, I almost believed that was what they were: some unidentifiable building supplies carelessly strewn about. I wanted to see them rise and slot into place, creating an enormous lattice of cream and white towering into the clear sky, waiting to be clothed with the flesh of stone and metal and concrete...

And then the feed cut off abruptly back to the spokesman's face, dispensing lies and prevarications. I silenced him and looked out the window again. The tower was gone. A plane crossed the empty sky.

•• · • · · • · · • · · • · ••

The buildings outside are brightly lit by streetlights, but nobody is in the ghost city. Only hungry ghosts. Like herself.

She squeezes the bony hand as contractions come on, uninterrupted. Isn't it strange that her famished body can contain so much pain?

••·•···•···•·••

I picked up my birth certificate and ran it through translation. I stared at the results for a long time. And then I called Muyang, our software engineer, who went by Mike.

"Sure," he said. "I can do it."

I sent him a scan of the document.

"It's a birth certificate issued by the Public Security Bureau's Household Registration Department," he said. "That's how it's done in China."

"What's the name?"

"Shen Jide. A nice name for a boy."

"A boy?"

"Yes. The child is male."

••·•···•···•·••

The agony is unbearable. Her body is being torn in two as the baby is forcing its way out. She digs her fingers into the bone, trying to divert pain with more pain. Something snaps, and a fingerbone of one of her dead midwives lies in her palm.

The sky is rosy red. Dawn? Sunset? She feels blood pooling around her legs, but cannot see it.

More clattering, clacking sounds. Voices whispering.

Ji.

•••••••••••

"Mum," I said. And then I was silent.

What could I ask her? *Mum, was I born a boy? Was I assigned male at birth? Who am I?*

"Jinnie..."

"That's not my name!" I yelled, surprising myself with the volume.

"It's as close as I could get."

"My original birth certificate says Jide. It means virtue, right? You could have called me Verity or something."

"It's not your name," my mother said, and her face on the video was flat and expressionless, as if it was receding into some distance where I could not follow. "It is the name of the boy who died."

•••••••••••••••

Holding the mewling package of warm flesh, she stumbles toward the door of the apartment: the door she had gone through centuries ago, or perhaps just a couple of hours ago. Now that linear time is restored, she thinks she can find it again.

The bony midwives let her out. They know what she is trying to do. They have been taking care of her for all those decades.

She tries to remember her name, but it slips away again. Her mind is as empty and flabby as her womb.

The baby whimpers. Inexpertly, she tries to tighten the swaddling she made out of her shirt. The baby is as tender as a bird's. The soft fold between its legs is like silk.

My daughter. Myself.

•••••••••••••••

"I came to China because it was my last chance," my mother said in the same toneless voice. "Adoption in the US was too long, too complicated, too costly. I wanted a baby. My marriage to your father was unraveling, and I thought a baby would keep us together. Stupid. Anyway, that orphanage in Guangxi arranged everything. They had a child for me, they said. A boy. That was unusual. It was mostly girls in the orphanages—one-child policy. Anyway, I was happy. I wanted a son, you see."

So, I was unwanted even by her.

"They showed me the child. As cute as a button. I got the certificate. And the next day, as I was getting ready for the flight back with my son, they called and told me he was dead. SIDS."

"So, they offered you a substitute. An inferior one. A girl."

"No, they did not. They did not have one. Chinese adoptions were all the rage then. I was heartbroken. I did not know what to do. So, I rented a car and drove to the new city that was built and abandoned in that district. Ghost cities, they were called. I just wanted something to distract me. To keep my mind off my failure."

She was silent for a while and then continued.

"It was the strangest place I had ever seen. Those immaculate streets, wide and clean. Fountains, plazas... And those towers rearing into the sky, glass and steel. And empty. Everything empty. I knew nobody had ever lived there, but the city still felt haunted. It was also soothing, somehow. I felt like I belonged with ghosts because I was not fully a human being. I could not give life. I was not alive. I lingered there until it started getting dark, and all the streetlights came on. The city was as bright as Broadway. What a waste! But the windows, the windows were all dark. And then a woman came out of one of these buildings. She was stumbling, and when she came closer, I saw that her pants were soaked in blood. And she was holding a baby."

"A baby."

"Yes. I wanted to ask her what happened, but I couldn't speak Chinese. Her face was smeared with blood, as if she were trying to clean herself up in the dark. She said, in English, "Her name is Ji."

And then she thrust the baby at me and went back into that huge, dark, empty building.

I stood there and knew I should follow, but I didn't. The baby was crying. It was a newborn. The mother had bitten off the umbilical cord.

It was a girl. I took her with me to the hotel; I had formula, diapers, everything. And I had the birth certificate for the boy, and the customs officials didn't care. So, I brought you home with me."

"Ji. Jinnie," I repeated dumbly. "So, that is my name?"

"I don't know," my adoptive mother said tiredly, as if the fatigue of all those years when she had tended a changeling suddenly dropped on her. "I don't know who that woman was. But I did look up the city afterward. There was nobody there. Nobody wanted to live there. It was the city of hungry ghosts."

•••••••••••

She is outside, and she hates it. The endless sky teeters over her, threatening to bury her under its weight. But the baby whimpers, and her cries spur her on.

Suddenly, she sees a figure walking toward her. It's so startling that she looks back with longing at the doorway of her tower. But she cannot go back in. Not yet. She needs to do something first.

The woman comes close, and in the harsh sunlight, her face is familiar and indecently young. Her blue eyes blink as she takes in the scene.

"What happened to you?" the woman cries.

She thrusts the baby at the woman. She wants to say she is hungry in the language they share.

"Ji," she says instead.

And rushes back into the tower, her refuge.

•• · • · • • • • · • · ••

It is a wonderful thing to live in a connected world.

I found images of my birthplace. The ghost city was still there. I stared, spellbound, at the eerie pristine towers against the luminous sky, white with pollution.

Guangxi. One of the areas where millions had starved to death. The place of hungry ghosts and walking skeletons. The ghost city of my birth was built on the site where the victims of Mao's Great Famine were buried in mass graves. China denies that this famine, in which 40 million died, even occurred. So, why not build a city on the site?

They should have known better. Hungry ghosts always come for you. And if they cannot rise because they lie buried under the weight of towers, they will send towers to haunt you instead.

They were still uncovering bones in the housing development next door. The internet was abuzz with gossip and speculation. But I knew where the bones had come from. I had brought them with me.

I did not need to call Mike again to find out what Ji meant. Hunger. As in *Jī huāng*, ⊠⊠.

Crop failure. Starvation. Famine.

I was born in the city of hungry ghosts. I *was* the city of hungry ghosts. And my birthplace was calling me back.

The tower was back. It blinked into being at sunrise and sunset, but was becoming present at odd times of day as well. It was as solid and palpable as the flat loops of highways and the crouching roofs of townhouses. It loomed over the sprawl—beautiful in its straight lines, its streamlined architecture, reaching for the sky with its promise of a bright new future. Housing for all. New age, new people, new city.

Nobody saw it but me, but it didn't matter. I knew I could reach it from anywhere. I knew the glass doors of its lobby would open for me. I could walk inside and then...

I would find my mother.

I did call the woman who had adopted me again, one last time. I wanted to know what my mother looked like.

"She looked like you," the woman said.

But I kept postponing it. Until the day I threw up in the morning. Until the day the pharmacy-bought test showed two blue lines.

•••••••••••

She steps forward as the glass door of the lobby swooshes behind her. From outside, the lobby looks brightly lit, but as she steps in, she plunges into thick, impenetrable darkness. It is so sudden that she thinks she's gone blind.

She looks back and through the plate glass, the streetlights blaze in their full glory over the empty sidewalk. But not a ray of light penetrates the building. A clacking sound comes from behind, and a bony hand touches hers.

"You are home," the voice says in the language she has never learned but somehow understands. "Come with us. We will take care of you, Ji."

"I am pregnant, and I need care for my baby. I know my mother is here. I want her to take care of me and her grandchild."

"Hunger consumes itself. Hunger consumes time. Here is no day and no night, no past and no future. You are your own mother, Ji."

SUCKER KISS LAKE

By Pip Pinkerton

"At Sucker Kiss Lake, when you need to get across,
If you want to get to the other side without taking a loss.
I suggest you go around, boat, or even fly,
Cause if you swim in the water, you're likely to die."
~ Local Children's Rhyme

PETE STANFORD WAS A man of simple tastes and pleasures. He worked a nine-to-five job at a tractor manufacturing company and owned a comfortable house less than a block away from a beautiful lake. Pete was happily married, with a wife who was neither comely nor homely, and two children, both of similarly outstandingly normal dispositions. He loved his children, but he never really felt like he knew them, or that they really knew him. He aimed to change that.

One of Pete's greatest pleasures in life was fishing. Today, the weatherman called for mild temperatures with a partly cloudy sky—a perfect fishing day. Pete decided to take advantage of this good fortune by bringing his two children out on Sucker Kiss Lake for a day of boating and fishing fun, and maybe for them to connect a little better.

By eight thirty that morning, they had loaded the boat into the water and were far away from shore, zooming across the lake, and leaving an intense white wave trailing in their wake. Pete was finally going to show his children his secret spot, the one his father had shown him when he was just a boy, the place where he had caught all his biggest and best fish. He slowed the engine as they neared.

"Drop the anchor, Adam," Pete told his seven-year-old son, who was sitting near the front of the boat. Adam braced his whole body as he bent down to lift the anchor up and over the side of the boat, causing a huge splash.

"You got me wet," Jessie complained loudly. She was two years older than Adam and intimidated him even though he was bigger than her. Jessie was sitting in the middle of the boat, in *her* spot. The middle was always Jessie's spot, and everyone mostly tried not to argue with her, as she was very particular about what she considered hers and prone to occasional boisterous protestations.

"Stop fighting, you two," Pete called from the back of the boat, next to the motor. He sniffed the air, breathing in the crisp breeze coming in off the lake. They were about sixty or seventy yards from the shore on the northern side, and about fifteen yards from the thick swampy area with all the lily pads and cattails. Pete knew he was in the right place as he could just barely see Camp Winnewog on the other side of the lake.

"Are we there yet?" Jessie asked.

"As a matter of fact, we are," Pete told his daughter. "Now, do you want minnows or crawlers?"

Pete only used minnows, worms, grubs, or night crawlers. He never used leeches. He refused to touch them. They felt like living slime between his fingertips, and holding them made his stomach lurch. The only time Pete had ever tried to use a leech, the slithery black devil, with no distinguishable body parts, slipped its slimy body out from between Pete's fingers and landed right on his upper thigh, just under the brim of his shorts. The leech felt like a huge, globby, slimy booger on his skin.

He had instantly reached down to grab the repugnant animal off his flesh and throw it far away from him, when he found, to his dread, the thing was stuck to his leg. That's when Pete screamed.

His father had rushed over to him, thinking the worst, realizing it was only the leech. He simply ripped it off and threw it into the water. Pete looked down at his leg, at where the leech had stuck to him, and there was an almost perfect circle, a little smaller than a dime, that was shinier than all the rest of his skin. A few beads of blood lined the edge. Pete had almost puked when he realized that the thing had been trying to eat him, and he became terrified when he realized he hadn't felt any pain, that one of those things could be on him at any time, slowly feasting away at him, and he wouldn't even notice. He had been afraid of leeches ever since.

"Minnows, please," Jessie said, staring at her father, breaking him out of his reverie.

Pete shook himself back into the present and looked at Adam. "You?"

"Same, please," Adam replied, looking over the edge of the boat into the murky water below. Adam had always been quiet, a kid who didn't like to stir the pot, completely the opposite of his sister. Pete had tried to break him out of his shell for the last year or two, but Adam was just a naturally quiet individual, an introvert in a family of extroverts.

Pete reached over and pulled up the little yellow minnow bucket so the opening was a couple inches out of the water. He dug his hand inside and pulled out a small, slippery minnow before reaching out and grabbing the hook at the end of Jessie's pole. He stuck the point of the hook into the minnow's mouth, forcing the curved metal through the small fish's body until it pierced violently through its side. He had pushed too hard, however, and the hook's barb point penetrated Pete's finger, causing him to bleed. He immediately stuck his finger in his mouth, realized where the hook had just been, then spat into the water. For just a moment, he watched his blood sink slowly down into the depths, never knowing that something was waiting just below, focusing on his dissipating blood even more intensely than he was.

A moment later, Pete cast his daughter's line before handing the rod back to her and helping her find the little, orange and yellow bobber floating uneasily on the water's surface.

Pete grabbed the other pole he had bought for Adam and repeated the procedure, casting the line on the other side of the boat so the kids wouldn't get tangled. Finally, Pete grabbed his own rod, put his favorite green and blue lure on the end of it, and cast his line out behind them, careful not to hit either of his children with the sharp hooks as he did so.

Not ten minutes after all three lines had been cast, the first fish took a nibble at the minnow on the end of Jessie's hook.

"Dad! Dad! I got a fish! I got a fish!" Jessie hollered ecstatically as her bobber plunged underwater and popped back up again. Pete stood up and moved slowly across the boat next to his daughter. He was ready to help if she needed it, or to take the fish off the end of the hook if she pulled the catch in by herself.

Jessie reeled fervently, the thrill of having a fish on the end of her line overwhelming all her other senses. The bobber was completely submerged, but the taut line zigzagged from side to side as the fish struggled to free itself from impending capture. Within seconds, the hunt was over as Jessie reeled in a small, greenish sunfish out of the water and into the cool mid-afternoon air.

Pete grabbed the fish, sliding his hand over the sunny's pointed back fins before reaching into his tackle box to pull out the all-purpose pliers. He gripped the hook, wiggling it back and forth inside the fish's mouth, pulling ever so slightly as he did so. A moment later, Pete dislodged the hook from the sunny's gullet.

"Can we keep it, Daddy? Can we?" Jessie asked hopefully.

"Yeah, can we?" Adam replied.

"Of course we can. That's what we came out here for," Pete said. He put his pliers back into his tackle box and retrieved a thin, blue-and-white-swirled stringer rope with a ring on one side and a sharp metal spear on the other. With the sunfish still in hand, Pete stuck the point of the metal rod into the sunny's mouth until it protruded out from under the fish's gill, then guided the pointed bar through the ring at the other end and pulled it through like he was threading a needle. Once the fish was secured on the stringer, Pete tossed it back into the water before tying the other end of the stringer rope to the side of the boat.

"Okay, guys. One down and a lake more to go," Pete told his children cheerfully.

Adam caught a fish five minutes later, and they just kept coming after that. Pete loved this much-needed quality time with his children, and his children enjoyed themselves just as much as he did, if not more.

They spent the whole day in their self-made bliss as the sky darkened without them realizing it. A chilly wind blew in from the east, giving Pete goosebumps up and down both arms. He was about to say something when his daughter spoke first.

"I'm cold, Daddy," Jessie grumbled. It was obvious that she wanted to stay out longer, but the nippy lake breeze was bothering her.

Adam had also started to shiver.

"Alright, guys, we should get heading back pretty soon," Pete said, having already drawn up the anchor and placed it in the bottom of the boat.

"No. Come on," Jessie cried. "Don't we have any blankets?"

"Please, Dad, just a little longer?" Adam asked.

Pete sighed. "Fine," he conceded, grabbing the gym bag under the seat, before putting the anchor back in the water, and withdrawing three heavy sweaters he kept in the boat, just in case. He knew how fast the weather on the lake could change.

Once everyone had their sweaters on, the mosquitoes seemed to find them.

"Have either of you seen my bug spray?" Pete asked his children.

Both kids gave similar half-shrugs.

Pete scanned the boat, trying to locate the small, green aerosol can before seeing it under Adam's seat, right next to his son's left foot.

"Adam, will you hand me the bug spray?" Pete asked, pointing to the can.

Adam, momentarily confused, picked up the bug spray and handed it in his father's direction. Pete couldn't quite reach it, and Jessie, always in the middle, didn't look like she was about to help. Pete leaned over his daughter, then stepped forward to close the distance, but when he put his sandaled foot down, he stepped onto a lure that he had somehow forgotten to put away. The fluorescent, green and orange, artificial fish bait twisted under the pressure of his foot, flipping its greedily sharp, triple hooks upward, tearing into the soft flesh near Pete's Achilles' tendon.

Pete screamed as the blood started to stream from his wound. He involuntarily jerked his foot upward, away from the pain, and as he did this, he realized his mistake. With one foot dangling, Pete began to tilt dangerously to the side. He slammed his foot down to maintain his balance, but his sandal landed directly on the anchor, the latch catching on the metal, and when he tried to dislodge himself, it only made the boat sway even more. Pete knew he was going overboard.

There was a tremendous splash as Pete sank into the icy-cold, murky depths of Sucker Kiss Lake. Unfortunately, he hadn't had much time to take a breath, so even though he was trying to remain calm, his body wasn't floating as effortlessly as he would have liked. While he was trying to find his bearings, another thought crossed Pete's mind, an idea somehow worse than not knowing which way was up. This thought made Pete panic and desperately need to get out of the water. He had begun to think about leeches.

Pete remembered all the stories he had heard over the years, the ones from his father, his father's friends, his own friends, the ones they all told after they had had too much to drink. His mind conjured up every repressed tale he could recall about the monster leeches that supposedly inhabited Sucker Kiss Lake, about people who had gone into the deep parts of the lake and came out looking blacker than midnight, with myriad leeches covering their entire bodies, about the rapacious nightmares that waited in the deep. All he had wanted to do was spend some time with his kids, to connect, to move on from the past. Besides, he had never really believed those tales anyway, at least not when he was above water.

Pete flailed his arms and legs, desperately trying to reach the surface against the weight of every article of clothing he wore, each seeming to add ten pounds as they dragged him down, pulling him further and further from the light, further from the fresh air that his burning lungs so desperately craved, further from the sound of Jessie's shrill, panicked screaming that was just now reaching distortedly to his ears, further from Adam's frantic calls and cries, further from hope.

Pete swam with all his might, and when it seemed like he would fill his lungs with air again, his progress was halted a mere six or seven feet from the surface. He looked down through squinted eyes, bending low and feeling around frantically with his hands. The anchor was connected to his shoe, and now, the chain had wrapped tightly around his ankle, and there was no way to free himself. Still, he tried, even though fire burned in his lungs and his fingers were numb with cold. His life was on the line, his children's safety; survival was the only option.

Pete was almost free of the anchor chain when everything suddenly went dark above him as something seemed to drown out his children's pleas and cries. Pete knew he only had precious little air left, but he looked up anyway.

Above him, an unnatural shape glided through the water, an abomination of serpent and shadow. Pete couldn't make out its features clearly, but he could tell it was bigger than any fish he had ever seen. The animal circled slowly around his trapped form as his eyes adjusted to the murky gloom. As the creature drew nearer, Pete realized the true nature of the huge, jet-black aberration that appeared to consist of nothing more than grim, stygian ink.

Pete turned away from the creature, refusing to believe what he was seeing. He craned his neck to look beyond the horror, toward the boat, and could barely make out Jessie's tiny, pink-manicured hand reaching into the water, grasping desperately at empty lake. Pete, momentarily forgetting that he was still attached to the anchor, swam determinately towards those tiny, grasping fingers, when they were blotted out once again by the abysmally black mass of smoothness headed straight at his face.

Pete watched helplessly as the black monster swam toward him, effortlessly cutting through the water and all too soon encompassing his entire field of vision. Pete closed his eyes as something reminiscent of cold, putrid Jell-O touched his forehead, before slowly starting to slime its way down his face. Pete couldn't take it anymore; his worst nightmare was coming true, the mother of all leeches had him in her clutches, and there was not a thing he could do about it.

Pete screamed, hoping to die. Instead of drowning, however, for no water rushed into his gaping mouth, he began to suffocate, as no air entered his lungs either. He instantly realized that the giant leech had his whole face in its suctioning maw, which caused an intense panic to overwhelm his entire being.

Pete threw his arms up, desperately trying to free himself from the creature, clutching and ripping at the slimy, rubbery flesh of the giant leech, but all to no avail. The leech secured itself to his face in a sucking kiss of death. Pete figured he had a better chance of ripping all the skin off his face than he did of dislodging himself from this monster's hungry embrace.

Pete's face went numb, like someone had overdosed him on anesthesia from the dentist. He felt euphoric. The burning in his lungs and the trauma of suffocating seemed far away and unimportant. It was like watching this nightmare scenario play out as if it were happening to someone else. The fear and the pain faded to distant memories, only to be replaced by an overwhelming sense of calm. Pete accepted that he was dying.

Pete felt the repulsive body of the giant leech slowly slither over his shoulders and around his torso. As much as it sickened Pete this malign animal's touch, he found a strange comfort in the leech's loathsome sepulchral embrace. At least he didn't have to die alone.

As the essence that was Pete Stanford faded from its body, his mind flooded with images of Adam and Jessie, of all his life's failures and accomplishments, his wife, his legacy, then nothing at all. Instead of creating memories with his children, he had created nightmares for them that they would keep for the rest of their lives, if they even got rescued, that is. Pete had drowned, entangled in the grip of his worst fear, made even worse by the fact that he was leaving his children to the unknown, even though he was only mere feet beneath their outstretched hands and crying voices, in the middle of Sucker Kiss Lake.

TOURIST TRAP

By Angus McIntyre

IT IS HOT IN the tunnel, a stifling heat that comes from nowhere and everywhere. The weight of the mountain presses down on me, holding me prisoner. My right arm is pinned against my side while I stretch my left out in front of me to grope for a point of purchase, something solid to push against, but I find only emptiness.

There is no light, nothing but the heat, the pressure, the choking closeness of damp air, the gritty feeling under my fingers, the thud of my pulse in my ears. I fight against the urge to scream for help. There is no one down here who can save me, and I am too afraid of what my screams will bring.

●•·•·••●••·•·••

"At least now we know where all the bananas come from," says Rose.

Steve stops and looks up. "Oh, yeah."

It seems odd to see bananas—still green and small, but recognizably bananas—growing from a stubby tree with broad leaves like a palm. I never thought about what a banana tree might look like or how bananas grow before they appear, yellow and uniform, in the supermarket.

I take out my phone and snap a picture, mentally captioning it for Instagram: "Actual banana tree. Lol." Before I put my phone away, I take another picture with Rose and Steve in it. Of course, I only really want Rose, but I can crop it later.

"I swear, if I eat another banana pancake, I'll turn into one," Rose says with an exaggerated sigh. Steve grunts in agreement. I say nothing.

Banana pancakes are breakfast fuel for backpackers. They're a fixture on every guesthouse and restaurant menu here, sugar-sweet rounds of yellow fruit wrapped in soft pancake dough, chased down with orange juice or coffee. An early morning sugar high to kickstart your day and get you moving before the growing heat turns you into a zombie and you give in to the urge to spend the day taking showers and sprawling on a lumpy dorm bed under a slow-turning fan.

Steve and Rose are Australian, but not, as I first thought, a couple. They only met in Vientiane, but they're both from Melbourne, which is apparently enough to establish a bond between them. Steve's doing his best to play up that sense of connection with the transparent goal of persuading Rose to have sex with him. Today looked like Steve's lucky day because Rose's friend Laura is in bed with a griping gut. Then I ended up tagging along, to Rose's evident relief and Steve's equally evident annoyance.

So here we are, standing on the bank of the Nam Song River, looking across dry rice fields toward a line of forested limestone mountains that rise steep from the floodplain, their jagged peaks fuzzed by heat haze and vegetation. Behind us, on the other bank of the river, lies the town of Vang Vieng; Population: who-gives-a-shit. Principal industry: feeding banana pancakes to foreign tourists. The rice fields are every shade of dry-season brown, chopped up into an irregular checkerboard by low walls of earth, the plowed furrows pointing the way to the mountains. Here and there are stands of banana trees with their pale green trunks and fringed green-and-yellow leaves, hung with clusters of ripening fruit in bunches, pancake ingredients of the future.

We follow a path of packed dirt that winds its way across the fields. Every so often we pass a little sign that says "Visit cave" or just "Caves," reassuring us that we're still going the right way. A bigger sign in questionable English promises us that a particular cave is "most beautiful and exiting" with "fresh hair." Competing signs try to lure us back to Vang Vieng, tempting us with alternative options: mountain biking, trekking, and tubing.

"You wanna go biking later?" asks Steve. The question is for Rose, not me.

"Maybe," she says.

•••••••••••••

Beyond the rice fields, the path climbs steeply, switchbacking up an increasingly steep hillside.

We stop and look out over the fields through a gap in the trees. Rose stands on a rock, shading her eyes with one hand. She has a bug bite on one leg, angry red against the smooth skin of her thigh, and a peeling sunburn on both arms. Her short blond hair glows in the sunlight. I squeeze my eyes shut against the brightness.

"Ready for some fresh hair?" says Steve. Rose nods, drops down nimbly from the rock.

The entrance to the cave is a little higher up. An old Lao man squats on his heels beside the opening, face like a wizened pixie, his cap of black hair shot with gray. He points to a sign with prices written in dollars, baht, and kip. He holds up three fingers. *Three dollars each.*

When we have all paid, he hands us each a headlamp and a chunky battery on a strap. The headbands of the lamps are stained black with sweat and mud. He shows us how to wind the bare end of the wire around the battery terminals. The lamps give off a weak yellow glow, barely visible in the daylight.

Inside the cave, they are more effective. Yellow circles of light reveal gray-white rock walls, the muddy floor printed with the soles of everyone who has come before us. Our guide pads in front on sandaled feet, stopping from time to time to warn us of slippery patches or low ceilings. He walks under one overhang almost without stooping, then turns and points at Steve and holds his hand over his head to indicate the difference in height. He mimes banging his head on the rock ceiling, his mouth open in simulated pain and surprise. He points to his eyes, then to the roof again. *Watch out.*

The winding passage is like an intestine with its bends and folds and whitish walls of moist clay. The air is not exactly fresh, but after the heat of the morning, it is pleasantly cool.

A little further on, the floor of the passage drops abruptly. There is a short ladder made of bamboo here, wedged in place between the walls. The passage is narrow enough that we must turn and descend the ladder backwards, our feet angled awkwardly on the slippery rungs. Beyond it, the passage slopes down more steeply.

I'm starting to feel claustrophobic. It's not a sudden panic but more a growing sense of dread. Bit by bit, I become aware of how much rock there is above us and how little it would take to block the slender lifeline that links us to the open air. I try not to think about the possibility of a cave-in. If we were trapped here, would anyone even know to look for us? And if they did, would they even be able to dig us out? Laos is starvation-poor; they'd probably have to send to Thailand for modern mining tools. Maybe they wouldn't want to dig at all for fear of setting off another collapse. Maybe they'd just seal up the entrance and leave us.

I distract myself by cataloguing impressions: the faint patterns left by moisture seeping down the walls, the gritty feel of the exposed rock when I run my fingers over it, the soft slap of the guide's sandals on the floor. The air is warmer again, and I'm sweating. Rose has taken off her T-shirt. My headlamp beam reveals the long line of her back, the ridge of her spine under brown skin, the curve of her waist, bikini straps floating over pale tan lines, fine golden down at the base of her neck. I admire the play of muscle in her calves as she descends the slope. I'm glad to have something other than the countless tons of fragile rock overhead to think about. Thoughts of sex are a welcome antidote to fear.

Even with Rose to distract me, my feeling of being trapped grows. The passage gets steadily smaller; we shuffle along with our heads bent, the beams of our lights sweeping the floor. From time to time, there are narrow sections that we must squeeze through one by one. The air that felt cool when we entered is now warm and thick, like wet rags clinging to my skin. It's hard to breathe, as if I'm sipping oxygen through a straw.

Just when I'm starting to wonder how much more I can stand, the passage opens up again. We've come to a dead end, the lowest point on our trajectory. Ahead of us is a teardrop-shaped cave with a ceiling high enough that even Steve can stand upright. The lower third contains a shallow pool of milky water, girdled by a miniature beach of golden sand. Our guide points, and in the dim light I glimpse a white shape in the water, a tiny fish that flicks its tail and disappears beneath a rock at the far end. Our headlamps cast their yellow circles on the surface.

"What's there?" says Steve, peering past us.

"Fish," says Rose.

"Where?"

"It's gone now," I say.

Steve wants to throw something in the pool to see if he can scare the fish into the open again, but Rose talks him out of it.

"What did it look like?"

"White. About this big," Rose tells him.

"Blind," I say.

He looks at me, his headlamp shining full in my eyes. "You know that for a fact?" he asks.

Of course it's blind, I think. It lives in a cave, in permanent darkness. What use would it have for eyes? But I don't say it.

"One crappy little fish," Steve says. There's a slight tremble in his voice. The cave is getting to him, too.

•••••••••••••

We're making our way out again when Steve finds the side passage.

"Hey, look at this."

It's easy to see why we missed it on our way down. It's barely wide enough to fit through, almost hidden behind a fold of rock.

"Can we go in here?" Steve calls back.

The guide shakes his head emphatically and points up the tunnel, saying something in Lao that none of us understands. He points again, to make sure that we get it.

"Oh, come on, just to look." Steve starts to squeeze through the crack. "Hey, there's a ladder here and everything. I'm going down."

The guide pushes past me, knocking my headlamp off. The wire pulls loose, and it goes out. I fumble in the darkness, trying to get it to work again.

"Rose, you have to come down here, it's really cool." Steve's voice floats up to us from somewhere below our feet.

"No. No." The guide speaks in a hoarse whisper, his creaky old-man voice sounding hollow and urgent.

"It's huge. And there are all these stalactites and stuff." There's a rattling, skittering sound from the opening, rock clattering on rock.

"No." The guide finds more English. "Wrong way. Wrong way."

"C'mon, man, just for a minute. Rose, get down here."

"You probably shouldn't," I say. I've managed to get my light working again. In the yellow circle, I see Rose leaning over to peer through the opening. "What if it's not safe?"

"You go back if you want, Matt," Steve calls. "This is too cool."

Rose shrugs, slips through the narrow opening. The old man reaches after her but pulls back at the last moment, as if he doesn't dare touch her. Her headlight beam sweeps across the ceiling of the tunnel as she climbs down the unseen ladder. "No, no," the guide says again. He turns and points at me, then points again up the tunnel. "Out," he says. His eyes are wild.

I hesitate, unsure what to do.

"Out," the old man says again, jabbing his finger at me. "Wrong way. You out."

I turn and start walking.

•••••••••••••

With only one lamp to light the way, the passage seems darker than before. I keep thinking that things are moving just outside the circle of my light, but whenever I turn my head, there's nothing there. It's still hot, the air taut and oppressive in the narrow space. Sweat trickles down my sides.

I hear noises behind me that might be voices, but the tunnel distorts sound. If they are voices, it's impossible to tell who's speaking or what they're saying.

I know I've blown it where Rose is concerned. I've been playing the nice guy: friendly, respectful, helpful, attentive. No pressure. I take care to let her know I'm not like that guy Steve with his macho antics. It's obvious enough what he wants, but I don't think Rose is down for it. I tell myself I'm still in with a chance.

Or at least I was. Now, it's just Rose and Steve, who went down into the *special* cave together, and me, Matt, who turned back because he was afraid. Matt, the good boy, doing what the guide told him to do. Matt, the coward, afraid of the dark and narrow spaces, and this sticky, suffocating heat. Matt, the loser.

Something clatters way back down the tunnel. I stop, listening. A brief fantasy flickers through my head: a sudden cave-in, the guide urging me not to go back, but then I courageously squeeze through the rockfall to free them; Steve, bruised and shaken, admitting that I'm the better man after all; Rose, frightened but miraculously uninjured, gratefully—

Then someone screams.

•• · • · • · •• · • · • · • · ••

I run crouched, stumbling, my elbows squeezed against my sides. My shoes slip on the muddy tunnel floor. I hold my phone in front of me, flashlight on. The blue-white glare of the LED reveals the tunnel walls in harsh black and white. Moisture glistens on the limestone walls.

I find the turn-off where the side passage opens up. There's no one there. I stick my head through the crack and wave my phone. Pendulous stalactites dangle from a shadowed ceiling, and rock fragments litter the cave floor below. At my feet is the top of a bamboo ladder. It's longer than the stubby ladders we climbed to get down here, a good ten or twelve feet tall.

"Rose? Steve?"

There's no answer to my shouts, only a confused murmur that might be voices or water or a falling rock.

The bamboo rungs of the ladder are polished smooth, and the ropes that lash the rungs together are frayed and dark with moisture. It's propped against the lip of the tunnel with nothing to hold it in place. I put my foot against it, and it shifts as I push. From somewhere below, there's a faint sound of scraping rock.

The battery indicator of my phone shows red. When I turn off the flashlight and drop it back into the pocket of my shorts, I'm plunged into darkness again. Only the topmost rungs of the ladder rise out of the black void.

I can turn back now, pretend I never heard anything, walk back up the tunnel, and wait for them by the cave entrance. Or I could wait here. It's probably nothing. Maybe Rose just got frightened in the dark. Even if they've run into trouble, it doesn't make any sense for me to go down there after them. The best thing I can do is to go get help.

I turn around and put my foot on the ladder.

•••••••••••••

The cavern is huge. I can see only fragments—thick limestone columns rising from a silty floor strewn with rubble, the tips of huge stalactites overhead, beads of water gleaming on the polished rocks. The ceiling is so far above me that I can't see it.

I can't understand why this isn't the main attraction. We crawled through narrow passages for what seemed like hours just to see a shallow puddle and a single sad little fish. Yet, there was this spectacular grotto right here. And the locals clearly know about it—the ladder is proof of that. So why hide it?

Because it's dangerous, says a voice in my head. *Maybe it's unstable. All they need is a few idiot tourists stumbling around down here to bring the whole thing crashing down.*

I remember the guide's whispered, "No, no." What if all it took to trigger a collapse was someone making too much noise? Someone like Steve, stamping around in the loose rock on the floor, shouting for Rose to follow him down the ladder.

I sweep my headlamp beam around, half-expecting to see the others buried under a fresh rockfall. Instead, I find more tunnels.

The entrances are no taller than my waist, the tunnels little more than burrows carved out of the rock. When I look closer, I can see what might be the marks of tools. Not metal tools but maybe stone, as if someone had used flints to chip away at the soft limestone, patiently turning a natural fissure into a passage large enough for a man to crawl through. But what were they digging for? Are precious gems or metal ores found in limestone? I try to remember, but draw a blank.

A sound comes from one of the tunnels, a weak muttering, like someone speaking.

I lift the headband to wipe the sweat from my forehead, then get down on my hands and knees and squeeze into the tunnel.

•••••••••••••

I find them on the other end of the tunnel. It's about twenty yards long, barely wider than my shoulders. I wonder how Steve even fit through here, or how he persuaded Rose to follow him.

It opens to a second cave. Again, I can't see the sides or the roof, but from the way the air currents move, it must be even larger than the first one.

The first person I see is the guide. He is on his knees, head bowed, his back toward me. He murmurs in Lao, words running into one another, repeating himself, hardly stopping to draw breath. I can't tell if he's praying or pleading, or both at once.

I find Rose next. She's crouching behind the conical trunk of a stalagmite, hugging it, her eyes tightly shut, her face pressed against the damp rock.

Steve lies face up on the cavern floor. When my light sweeps over him, I see what they've done to him.

It isn't the mutilated body on the cave floor that holds my attention, though.

There are pale shapes in the darkness, their outlines indistinct. When the light touches them, they turn in unison toward me, their eyeless heads moving as one. They are human-sized, but there's nothing human about them. Their unnatural musculature is sharply defined beneath the translucent skin. One of them creeps forward, head moving from side to side as if listening for something. It holds its long, clawed hands close to its chest. When it opens its jaws, I see the black tunnel of the mouth, lined with peg-like teeth that can rasp stone.

They are all around us. They crouch on the floor of the cavern, their long limbs unfolding slow as dreams. One is close enough that I can see the quick pulsation of its throat. Dark stains spatter the sides of its head. A snakelike tongue flicks out, tasting the air.

Rose opens her eyes. She releases her hold on the stalactite and crawls toward me, agonizingly slow. I creep backward on my heels, feeling for the mouth of the tunnel behind me with one hand.

Her foot kicks a loose rock. The sudden clatter is like an explosion in the oppressive silence.

The creatures move all at once.

●•·●·•·●•·•·●·•●

I don't know where Rose is. We fled together while they ate the guide, scrambling through the tunnels on all fours, scraped and bloodied by the rough rock walls. When we emerged into the first cave, they were waiting for us.

From my hiding place, I hear them hunting her. They fill the darkness with grunts and little yipping cries, punctuated by a throaty chuckle like laughter. It sounds as if they are playing with her, chasing her from tunnel to tunnel in the dark, letting her stumble a little way ahead only to ambush her again. When they grow tired of the game, it will be my turn.

I squeeze myself further into the crevice I have found. My headlamp is gone, lost somewhere in the labyrinth of tunnels under the mountain. The blackness around me is absolute, but they do not need light to find me.

The cramped space squeezes the breath out of me, compressing my lungs. It feels as if the whole weight of the mountain is bearing down on me. Each time I inhale, it tightens a little more. There's no air to be had here anyway, only a thick, warm vapor that smells of them, laden with fine particles of sand that cling to the inside of my throat as I fight to breathe.

I go limp, stretching myself out as far as this narrow grave will permit. I am past struggling now. Even if I could free myself from this narrow cleft in the rock, even if I could somehow find my way through the stone maze to the place where we entered, they will never let me leave.

So I lie still, sipping a few last breaths of stale air through sand-choked lungs, and wait for them to come for me.

LIGHTS OUT

By Edward Ahern

"YOU'RE GOING TO DO what?"

"Strap you down with what amounts to a lie detector wired onto you, then completely blacken the room. Completely."

"But why, Professor Givens? I already told you I'm afraid of the dark."

"Jack, unfortunately, we get a lot of students who'll say anything to make eighty dollars a session. Before we can proceed to the experiment, we need to verify that you do have nyctophobia."

"Hah?"

"Nyctophobia. Fear of the dark. Named for the Greek goddess Nyx, who—oh, never mind, the qualifying test takes five minutes once you're rigged up."

"Do I get paid for the qualifier?"

"Twenty dollars."

Jack edged further back in his chair. "What about a nightlight or maybe instrument lights?"

Givens let out a dry chuckle. "You know, there are almost as many night lights in this country as there are people. Not counting all the constantly burning yard, garage, and walkway lights. As a species, we really do fear the dark. No, Jack, no light at all for five minutes. But you can stop any time you want. You'll be holding a panic button, and if you press it, the lights come back on."

"But only twenty dollars?"

"For this trial. But during the real experiment, you'll be well paid for a half hour in the dark."

Jack exhaled. He needed the money. "Okay, let's do it."

Givens smiled. "That's the spirit. But it wouldn't be a university experiment without a questionnaire. So it's question time. Question one: When do you first remember being afraid of the dark?"

"I was always afraid. And my mother's mother, who used to babysit, was vicious about it. She used to recite an old poem to me about the bogeyman.

"Do you sleep in the dark now, Jack?"

"Never. Two lights, so when one bulb goes out, I have another still lit."

The questioning went on for ten minutes. Givens eventually clicked off the recorder. "We can do the test now, if you like."

"Uh. Okay."

Givens led Jack into an adjoining room. The room was windowless, bare except for a reclining chair and an EKG machine on a wheeled dolly.

"Take off your shirt, Jack, and sit erect in the chair. Once I've set you up with pulse, respiration, and skin monitors, please lie back and get comfortable."

"Doubt I'll be comfortable. I've already started to sweat."

Once Jack was rigged and ready, Givens handed him a wooden cylinder with a wire coming out of one end and a depressible button on the other. "It's, pardon the expression, a dead man switch. Hold it down throughout the session. Once you release it, the test is aborted, and the lights come on. But if you release it before we've completed our readings, we'll have to send you home without pay and find a new applicant."

Jack settled back in the chair, and Givens left the room. A few seconds later, the room speaker clicked on. "Okay, Jack, here we go."

The room went black. Jack began to softly whine, the same monotonal noise he'd used as a small child to protect himself from the dark creatures. But he stopped, embarrassed that Givens was listening to him panic. And it was panic. The air around him eddied and flowed as if things swam in it.

Jack squeezed his eyes shut and clenched his fists, his knuckles cracking. Thousand one, thousand two, he began. Five minutes was a count to three hundred.

Something brushed against his right trouser leg, and he almost dropped the panic button, but he held on. Jack's armpits had gone squishy with rank sweat. "Thousand seventy, thousand seventy-one." Jack was counting out loud now, not caring that Givens heard.

Something was in the room. He sensed it, knew it. Something that was released when the blanket of light was pulled away. It was to his right, waiting. "Thousand one sixty, thousand one sixty-one." *God*, he thought, *help me through this. You are of the light; hold this at bay.*

But there was no answer, and no light. “Thousand two ten, thousand two eleven.” Jack felt tiny touches on his arms and legs, as if mites were crawling up and disturbing his body hairs. He scratched at himself until he was sure he'd drawn blood.

As he moved his arms and legs, he felt resistance like something had nestled up against him. “Thousand two ninety-eight, thousand two ninety-nine, thousand three hundred. There! I've done it!”

He threw the panic button off the chair to his right, hoping to hit whatever it was. The lights snapped back on, and Jack looked around the room. Nothing. He saw long, angry scratches on his arms and legs. Givens came into the room, a polite and probably insincere smile shaping his mouth.

“Well, your count was a little fast, but we got our readings. Congratulations. We can proceed to the test.”

“I don't want to do it. Take this stuff off me, please.”

Givens began popping off suction cups and removing the blood pressure cuff and respiration strap. “Jack, we can't do the experiment without you. If it's the money, I can double your stipend.

You've suffered with this all your life; don't you want to learn more about it?"

"I'm scared, Professor. There, I've said it."

Givens stared down at Jack for a few seconds. "You know, Jack, I can't think of much better protection than what you have here. I'll be closely monitoring you and your vitals from just outside the room. That's got to be better than a ten-dollar night light."

It was Jack's turn to stare. His car sat in the dorm parking lot, undrivable until it got two hundred fifty dollars' worth of life support. "I'm going to need three hundred dollars. Firm."

Annoyance flickered across Given's face, then the unctuous smile reappeared. "Okay, Jack, I'll make an exception. But we'll need to do the trial tomorrow morning. Would that be all right?"

Tomorrow was Saturday, so no classes, and Jack wanted it to be over.

"Okay, sure."

"Come at eight-thirty. There are some things I need to explain to you."

On the way back to his room, Jack speed dialed Suzie. "Suz, I need company. And some of that warm care you provide. Couple beers at Stan's?"

"You sound shaky, Jack. Everything okay?"

"Not so much. But I'll tell you when I see you."

Stan's draft beer was cheap and almost flat, but it did the job. Halfway through the second beer, he opened up. "So there it is, Suz. I'm afraid of the dark."

"Not a huge surprise. Your damn lights keep me awake. But Jack, bogeymen aren't real. Even if they were, it's like they're restrained from getting at us."

"Yeah, I guess."

Suzie continued. "It's only going to last half an hour, and the butthead professor will be eavesdropping the whole time. You'll get freaked, but my guess is that you can do it. And it would be nice for you to have wheels again."

"Selfish bitch."

"And you love me for it."

"Stop by the dorm?"

"What an enticing proposition. But no, I've got a paper to finish. Call me in the morning before you get strapped in."

Jack stopped for service-truck Mexican on the way back to his room, exchanged trash talk with his roommate, and went to bed. He surprised himself by sleeping well, but anxiety struck him as soon as the alarm clock went off.

Jack understood, logically, that his fear was irrational, but he feared beyond reason that he did not belong in a dark place. He dressed and left.

"Hello, Jack. A bit late, aren't you? No matter. Let me explain some things to you while I rig you up."

Givens led him back into the room with the reclining chair and showed him a large, many-dialed unit that fed wires to what looked like lightbulbs from the 1800s in corners of the room.

"What's that?" Jack asked.

"A light machine. Sit back down, Jack. There you go. We're evaluating a hypothesis. We initially ran tests with subjects who had no fear of the dark, but the results were disappointing."

"Disappointing?"

Givens applied straps and suction cups as he spoke, "It's complicated, but let me explain in non-scientific terms. Darkness is usually defined as the absence of light, but light is weird stuff. We can also produce darkness by overlapping light waves that cancel each other out. We can produce darkness *with* light, and that's what we're going to do today."

Givens adjusted a metal fiber skull cap onto Jack's head.

"What's that for?"

"To give us a better idea of what you're seeing or not seeing. We can't just rely on your descriptions. Anyway, the overlapping light waves will produce a completely dark area. And that area can move faster than light."

"Nothing can move faster than light."

"Almost nothing, Jack. The overlapping waves create an effect similar to the cutting action of a pair of scissors. The action itself is twice as fast as the movement of an individual blade. With me so far?"

"I guess."

"That's where you come in, Jack. Our instruments tell us a lot, but not the apparent effects of this overlapped darkness. You're hyper-sensitive to the dark, and we need your subjective feedback. There, I think you're rigged and ready." Givens stepped back from the chair and gave Jack his billboard smile. "I'm going to lower the chair back and lock it in position so your field of vision is limited to the dark area we're going to generate. I'm also going to strap down your torso and head so you can't move away from that field."

"But the room will already be dark, isn't that enough?"

"Not nearly. We'll first remove all light, just to eliminate any distractions for you. Then we'll generate the field and let you sense what you can. If anything."

"But I get the panic button?"

"Oh, absolutely. Uh, Jack, you did relieve yourself before you came in?"

"Yes."

"Excellent." Givens finished tying Jack down and tried but failed to move Jack's body and head. "Very good. We'll start shortly. Here's the dead man switch. I'd wish you luck, but I'm sure you'll do well."

Givens turned a little too quickly and left the room. Jack had begun to sweat while Givens was talking, and droplets trickled down his forehead. The lights cut off, and darkness dropped on Jack like a heavy duvet. "Thousand one, thousand two," he began, wondering how he could focus on observing while he was counting.

Servo motors in the large machine behind him came to life, and a high-pitched whining drowned out Jack's counting. Harsh, glaring cones of light formed above and behind him, then gradually overlapped and mutually dimmed until darkness was again complete.

And more. The blackness in front of him seemed more substantial, more deeply inky. Jack squeezed his eyes shut, then realized that Givens could probably tell when his eyes were closed, and cautiously reopened them.

The whine of the machinery syncopated with another noise, a rasping that seemed to come from the ebony ichor in front of him. "Thousand thirty-eight, thousand forty," he mumbled.

Odors drifted past him, the rank, fetid smells of plants and animals long dead in a bog. The grating in front of him condensed into almost syllables, almost words. The darker area appeared to heave.

Jack began screaming, "Thousand hundred ten! Thousand hundred eleven! My God, I can't do this!" His bowels opened, and he soiled himself as he kept screaming.

He released his thumb from the dead man's switch, but the room stayed dark, the whines and screeches howling. A vague, velvety form slithered toward Jack as if swimming against the current of the light waves. Jack lost his ability to scream and sat open-mouthed, half-gargling sounds from the back of his throat.

The amorphous blackness touched Jack's shoes, then crab-walked over his pant legs and his genitals and torso. Jack fell silent, catatonic. He strained against the bands holding him and then sagged.

Givens reentered two minutes later, his lips pressed together, his nose wrinkled at the smells.

"You gave us a bit of a scare, Jack. Your readings were frantic, but you seem to have stabilized nicely. I'm sorry about the dead man switch, but we needed to test your reactions in a panic situation. Please don't be mad at us. Jack, say something."

"I'm… acclimating."

"Thatta boy, Jack. Take your time. We'll get you cleaned up. Wow, what a display you put on. Do you feel okay? Your brain wave patterns changed radically. Would you like some water? Are you still afraid of the dark?"

"I am free."

Givens frowned. "Free? So you no longer fear the dark?"

Jack's face was expressionless. "Free to live."

Givens released Jack's restraints, and Jack swung down from the chair and stepped close to Givens. The smells of feces and something else—rot maybe—were acrid.

"You will conduct this test with others who fear the dark?"

"With your success, absolutely. There are several already scheduled."

Jack half smiled. "So the barrier will be removed many times."

"Your ability to face your fears will encourage us to proceed, Jack. You should be proud."

"I no longer fear the dark." Jack smiled with his lips but not his eyes. "But you should."

WALLFLOWER

By Juliette Jarabek ~ "To those who read this; I love you."

LORELEI SWUNG THE DOOR shut as quickly as she had opened it, praying the hinges' sharp squeals would be drowned out by her hunters' piercing howls and thundering footfalls. Back against the door, she clutched the front of her blouse in a white-knuckled grip, as if to smother her racing heartbeat. Eyelids screwed shut, she slapped her free hand over her mouth and nose. She could not concern herself with the blood seeping from her cut hand, staining her pallid, sweaty face; what mattered was keeping her fearful whimpers locked away as the wild stampede savaged the hallway she had just narrowly escaped.

Whatever pursued her rushed and rioted past the sleek, aged door like a train, and Lorelei could feel the floor shake and twitch from the hellish force. A cacophony of brutish hissing, clawing, and hooting resounded endlessly through the door, threatening the very integrity of the manor's ancient walls as the noise, wholly inhuman yet too malevolent to be purely animalistic, pushed tears from her sealed eyelids. The seconds lasted an eternity before the lamented clamor slowly faded, waning until there were only the lingering echoes of adrenaline and desperation. She idled in the black sanctuary behind her eyelids for one precious moment more before willing herself to crack them open and return to her reality.

It did not take long for her eyes to adjust; darkness plagued what appeared to once be a sitting room, now a cadaver of what it once was, visible only by the moonlight leaking through lace curtains. What sparse light existed could only illuminate what was immediately in front of her, as mountains of antiques, knick-knacks, doodads, and general junk obstructed her view.

Thick coats of dust blanketed the surfaces of dressers, mirrors, and boxes, all left to decay. The walls were withering, the musty wallpaper a relic of comfort and safety—ironic, considering the faded floral pattern twining about its curling, yellowed lengths. Lorelei made painful discoveries as she haphazardly navigated the room, bumping her thigh on the edge of a coffee table, her shoulder against the side of a bookshelf, her hip into the arm of a bergère chair. Between the blooming bruises across her body and the throbbing slice in her palm, she struggled not to inhale more dust with her wheezy sniffling.

Those soft cries caught in her throat as she heard something, a shock and shudder shooting up and down her spine as the airborne dust became the least of her concerns. *A creak, slow and shrill.* Lorelei recognized it immediately—the warning call of the door, the room's only entrance and exit. Worse still, following the suffocating silence, her blood-hot ears picked up the quick, skittering drag of long limbs against the wood floor and plush carpet.

Lorelei had to move quickly, quietly, and *now.*

She shimmied, shifted, and shirked, twisting and mangling herself between rogue chairs and packages disregarded decades ago, all to avoid alerting whatever else now stalked the stacks with her. In the stillness of this strange territory, every sound she made felt amplified, and the fear that someone—*something*—would hear her and come back while she was struggling, always running the risk of making a wrong turn and pinning herself somewhere she could not escape, made her anxious panting even more persistent. The ceiling was concerningly low, even for a short woman like her, practically echoing back her every step when her foot met hardwood flooring instead of carpet.

The cramped quarters slowed her down, as the labyrinthian pathways grew narrower and narrower, boxes spread more sporadically, threatening to trip her or clatter to attract the attention of whatever was following her. She flinched every time she risked knocking down one of the heavy, rotting cardboard towers. Considering her stout figure, she had to squeeze past all the precarious pieces of furniture, décor, and God knew what else. She was overheated, dizzied, nauseous, and frenzied—a spiraling kaleidoscope of panic, distress, and malaise.

Stack upon stack, pile upon pile—the hoard was stifling, never-ending. The towers only grew taller with every turn, every push through continuously constricting passageways. Whether she was chasing salvation or fleeing horror, Lorelei desperately hoped, begged whatever higher power existed, that there was somewhere she could go, something she could do, if she went deep enough into the room's recesses. The atmosphere grew continuously more oppressive the further she shoved herself through endless stacks of boxes, air thick with the heavy, acrid smell of mold, neglect, and stale perfume.

Could that thing smell *her*, too? Her sweat? Her blood? Her fear?

Further and further and further and further—spaces only tightened around her until boxes and furniture practically strangled her, stubbornly trying to hold her in place. She had long since stopped caring if anything tore her skirt and blouse; so long as she kept moving forward, that was all that mattered...

Until she felt something brush against her, a teasing, fleeting touch. It was rough and thin, and after its initial contact, it returned with force. Confident, determined, it curled around her ankle, anchoring her in place. She glanced down in panic, kicking her ankle in an attempt to dislodge it.

However, the tendril only tightened its hold, slithering up Lorelei's calf and squeezing her flesh. Another vine grabbed her wrist, its length advancing in a tight curl down the meat and tendon of her hand. The sharp tip trailed along the palm's curving life line until it gently brushed against her bloody, beading wound, as if offering a soft, cold kiss. Then followed a third coil around her forearm, then a fourth, a fifth, a sixth. More wormed their way around her joints, stifling and tight before they began to *pull*, guiding her protesting body forward.

Tears she had fought to contain finally broke, rolling down her sticky cheeks as she continued to resist. Lorelei no longer cared about making noise, knocking over surrounding debris as she thrashed and flailed. Her wide green eyes traced the vines, trying to track their origin, and with a sob, she found it—*the wallpaper*. A pulsing mass of roses, peonies, stems, and leaves flourished outward from the nearest wall, growing larger and larger with each breath, eating up what little space was left as Lorelei tried to get away.

One of her loafers touched the living, beating blooms, their petals caressing the scuffed leather as her feet and legs were dragged *into* the wall. Lorelei's mind raced with panic, her body paralyzed as her lips trembled and mumbled pleas that only the room could hear, witnessed only by whatever else may have been hiding in wait around each corner. The creeping plants trailed their way around her body like rope, holding her tight and snug as she was engulfed through the petals, the filaments, the ovary—inward until her grunts and wails were consumed in one botanic embrace.

BROKEN AND BONDED, DOOMED AND PARDONED

By Ilan Jones ~ "For Amber, Faelan, and Vidar."

AN HOUR AFTER THE argument and the image of Claire's eleven-year-old daughter's tear-filled eyes still lingered in her thoughts. Her own words gnawed at her stomach. She wished she could take it all back. Claire hoped one day Julia might understand why she worked so tirelessly. All she wanted was to give her daughter a normal life. She doubted now if she ever could.

She dabbed a finger at her mascara. Her coworkers would gossip if they saw that she had been crying again. Most of them hated her guts anyway. At least she had arrived late enough that the elevator was empty. She chewed the side of her thumb. She hated being late. She had used up her boss's sympathies during her divorce. She couldn't afford to get written up again.

She would deserve it, too. It wasn't Julia's fault for missing the bus. Claire was to blame. It didn't matter that traffic was so terrible that she abandoned her cab to walk the rest of the way. The problem was her. She failed at everything. Marriage, parenting, and work, she always found ways to screw it up. Claire cursed herself for being so negative, but she couldn't shake the feeling that she was coming into work only to be fired.

The elevator doors slid open with a robotic voice declaring she had arrived at the twenty-fourth floor. The lobby was empty, quite abnormal for a Tuesday morning. Deeper into the suite, Claire heard voices near the meeting rooms. She turned a corner and found the entire office huddled around three large conference screens.

"What's going on?" she whispered.

"Haven't you heard?" said another employee. "The world is ending." Claire searched the woman's red-rimmed eyes for humor in vain. She scanned the room for her manager, but she was nowhere to be seen. Many of her coworkers clung to one another, their tear-stained faces had become twisted masks of grief. While others appeared bereft of any emotion at all, their blank stares and ghostly pallor were the only expressions of their disbelief. Someone raised the volume above the hushed whispers and open sobbing echoing from every corner of the room.

Chaos unfolded across the displays. The disparate voices of news anchors collided into a babbling mess, with only the occasional word or phrase making it through, like "Global Catastrophe," "confused scientists," "blood rain," "mysterious entities," and "please stay in your homes."

"Oh, God," a woman screamed nearby. "It's happening here." The crowd shoved Claire aside in their wild dash across the office to the large windows overlooking the street. She stayed near the back, watching as a once sunny day turned bleak and dim like an eclipse. Outside, a strange sound like the rending of some enormous sodden carpet shook the building's walls.

"Look," a man shouted, "The sky is splitting just like on TV!" Claire watched in mutual horror as a mile-long gash splintered down the middle of the roiling black sky. The edges of the seam glowed red and dripped like magma discharged from the depths of the Earth. A collective cry went up as the split burst apart into a hideous wound spewing torrents of sticky red rain over everything.

"It's blood," an inconsolable woman shouted. "It's blood just like everywhere else." Before anyone had thought of moving away from the windows, the elevator doors closed with Claire inside. She needed to get to Julia. She had to save her daughter. She was trying frantically to call Julia's cell when the lights went out and the elevator stopped, knocking her to her knees. Her phone disappeared into the blackness of the elevator. She searched desperately on all fours until her fingers landed upon what she knew to be her phone. Turning it over, the screen brightened, but remained blank; the glass shattered. She sobbed, thinking of what to do next.

Claire shone the dim light of her phone on the elevator's emergency call button. It made no sound when pressed. The power was out. Not even the standby generators had turned on. Images of the elevator suddenly plummeting to the ground with her inside raced through her mind. Her chest tightened.

Her fingers wriggled into the gap in the door. Her arms ached as she pried the halves apart. The elevator had stopped between floors. She saw the shadows of people running by the small crack at the top of the door. She cried for help, but nobody stopped. The slightly taller gap between the bottom of the door and the ceiling of the next floor was her only chance. The opening was small, but she might be able to slide her shoulders through if she tried. With a bit of luck, she would fit the rest of her body through as well.

Claire put her phone inside her purse and tossed it through the opening with her other belongings. She tried to arrange her coat so that it might cushion the eight-foot fall on the other side. She lay down on the elevator floor and pushed her head through the door. The hallway was deserted. For a moment, she watched the bloody rain run in rivulets down the windows facing her. Something large pressed itself against the glass. Her breathing quickened. How could any of this be happening? How could this be real? Julia must feel so alone right now. The thought of her terrified daughter spurred her on.

Claire slid one arm out and had enough room to fit her other hand, but it was tight. She shut her eyes to the great shifting shapes on the other side of the glass and contorted her body, trying to free herself from the elevator. After a brief struggle, she pulled her other arm through without losing too much skin. She dreaded what was to come.

She pressed herself as hard as she could into the narrow opening. Her legs slid uselessly against the elevator floor. Pain coursed through her as she wrenched her torso through almost past her breasts. She was stuck. She couldn't breathe. The opening was too tight around her rib cage, and she had used up the strength of her arms. She would suffocate if she couldn't break free. She thrashed like a trapped animal.

The edges of her vision darkened. Long, misshapen cables of flesh moved like hungry worms on the other side of the glass. Some were the size of vines, while others were as thick as tree trunks. The occasional fleshy appendage slithered across the glass, looking for somewhere to take root. A sound like a trumpeter's call mixed with the rage of a hydrogen bomb filled the air inside and out.

Claire covered her ears against the deafening noise. The windows shattered in unison, launching broken glass and blood into the hallway. The vibrating elevator loosened around her chest, freeing her from its grasp. She fell headlong onto the hard, wet floor, where she writhed, gasping for air. The elevator car, free of its passenger, careened into the darkness below.

Fighting against the pain of the fall, Claire pulled herself up and staggered down the hallway with her belongings. She reached the stairwell. Throwing open the door, she joined the building's hundreds of other occupants in their stampede to escape. She anchored herself to the handrail as the heaving mass of people propelled her down the stairwell.

The heat of the pressing bodies made her delirious. She thought she might faint or vomit. Soft things squished underfoot. She clung to the handrail ever tighter when she felt their clawing fingers or heard their muffled cries. The building shook terribly, and the awful trumpeting continued, mingling with her coworkers' screams.

She followed the main body of the crowd into the ground-floor lobby, while others carried on to the parking garages below. She could barely hold herself upright against the violent vibrations that threatened to bring the building down on top of them. Cries from the collapsing stairwell behind her pushed her to move ever faster.

She hurtled out the doors into a world gone mad. The dim glow of streetlamps lit the way through torrents of falling blood. The city was nothing short of a nightmare. The immobile skeletons of cars choked the devastated streets. The horrendous wailing in the heavens began once more. Claire couldn't stifle her screams upon witnessing the source of the world's sudden descent into madness.

The tear in the sky had grown larger. Its center birthed huge masses of seething veins and other lashing viscera. Their twisting coils crashed down to earth, obliterating everything in their path. An enormous artery snaked around a scuttled metro bus and lifted it skyward. Another collided with a skyscraper, sending a cloud of rubble upwards to be devoured by the voracious sky.

Claire sought cover as the howling took on a new pitch, heralding the arrival of a new horror. A mass of chitin festooned with innumerable eyes forced its way through the laceration. Its cries at once captivated and terrified her. The atrocity's birth brought back memories of the day her daughter came into the world. She remembered Julia's face smeared with blood and vernix. She was the most beautiful thing in the world.

She bolted towards Julia's school, but the carnage unfolding all around her made the journey painfully slow. Claire dodged falling debris as she raced over broken asphalt, twisted cars, and the remnants of dead human beings. One of the ravening veins erupted from the ground behind her. She dove towards the open rear door of a nearby taxi, rolling her ankle as the heel of her shoe snapped in the desperate lunge for the safety of the backseat.

Inside the cab, Claire eased the door shut with a hand over her mouth to suppress the pain and conceal her location. Her leg throbbed as she cast off her shoes, cursing herself for not taking them off sooner. She still had at least twenty blocks to go before she would even set eyes on the gray bricks of the middle school, but she couldn't move.

The taxi reminded her of her commute that morning. It could have been the same cab for all she knew. Julia would have ridden the bus and Claire the train, but the night before, Julia had snuck around the apartment playing games and chatting with her friends online. Of course, once caught, it ended in a fight like always.

Julia blamed her for everything wrong in their lives: the small apartment, the change of schools, and especially Tom's leaving. Claire blamed herself, too, not for how he left on a "Business Trip" with his accountant only to mail her divorce papers from Maui, but for not having the courage to tell Julia the truth about her philandering father. The bastard didn't have the decency to tell his own daughter goodbye. His only interaction with her during the past two years had been through his lawyer and monthly child support deposits.

Claire wanted so badly to tell Julia that it wasn't her fault, but the timing was never right. She refused to address it in the heat of an argument, and the fragile times of peace in her home were so rare that she dared not break them. She should have handled it long ago, but she was afraid that when the truth did come out, it would only cause her daughter more harm. So much for that.

Her daughter needed her more than she needed rest or safety. She had to make things right. Claire bolted from the cab, leaving her shoes behind. She ignored the pain in her ankle. Though the blaring roars of the creature overhead and the constant sight of human remains gnawed at her sanity, she did her best to overcome the obstacles in her path. The constant terror of being crushed by falling debris or swept up in great bloody coils of the beasts was beyond even her worst nightmares. She prayed Julia wasn't seeing this. She couldn't let her go through this alone.

She had only ten more blocks to go. Her lungs felt like they might burst. Her legs and feet burned as if on fire. For the first time, Claire turned to see the destruction she had fled. A quaking mass of blood and sentient organs had consumed downtown. The many-segmented body of the mewling beast in the sky had nearly reached the ground. Its innumerable eyes blinked in and out of existence, emitting a reddish glow through the already red mist that hung over everything.

Claire had lingered too long. The hungry tissues of the creature descended toward her in their all-devouring quest. The meat-covered streets closed in around her. She had to escape. Running to a sinkhole, she discovered that it connected to the sewer below. The awful stench of human waste and discarded grease was overwhelming. Blood mingled with wastewater to rush away in the direction of the school. She had nowhere else to run.

Claire traversed broken slabs of asphalt down into the sewer. She plunged into the foul currents and fought her reflexes to keep from vomiting in the fetid dark. She drew her phone from her purse and prayed for it to work. After some coaxing, it sprang to life. The dull light of its broken screen only illuminated a foot or so in front of her.

She trudged as quickly as she could through the swirling stream. The low ceiling of the sewer forced her to walk hunched. She held a hand firmly over her nose and mouth to stop herself from screaming every time some unseen thing brushed against her legs. Her pulse rang in her ears, and the smell of sulfur was upon everything. In the dark, her panic grew at the thought that she might never find the school.

At last, she saw the faint glow of four columns of light up ahead. She charged forward and found the rusted rungs of a ladder set into concrete, leading up to a manhole cover. She was at an intersection. Only nine more of these ladders, and she would be there. The anticipation of leaving this disgusting place was too much. As she propelled her exhausted body through endless filth, she tried to mentally escape, thinking back to the events of that morning.

•• · • · • • • • · • · ••

"You only care about your stupid job," Julia shouted. "That's why Dad left."

"That's not true." Claire didn't want to fight; she was so tired of fighting. "Please, can we just hurry up and go?"

"No, I'm not going anywhere. Not until you admit it. Not until you admit that you love your job more than you love me."

"Julia, please."

"No. You hate me. I know it. Just admit it. You hate me just like you hated Dad, and that's why he left." This hadn't been the first time Julia had made this accusation in a fit of preteen anger. She couldn't bear to hear it for another time.

"Fine," Claire snapped. "I hate you. Does that make you happy?" The girl's mouth moved as if to speak, but no words came out. "Every time I see your ungrateful, rotten face, I am reminded of your two-timing father who chose to spend the rest of his life with a slut from his office instead of with us." Julia's lip quivered. Claire had lost all sympathy in that moment. The memory of her words pained her. She should have kept her mouth shut.

"I hate that the life I had is gone, and all that's left for me is to slave at a job that makes me miserable for my selfish brat daughter, who only wishes me dead. I hate having to wake up every morning knowing I'll be attacked for doing the right thing."

"Mom, I..." Claire had never seen such pain in Julia's eyes before, but there was no taking it back. The girl's anguish tore at her own heart, but she couldn't show it. Not now. All she wanted in life was to be a good mother, and in an instant, she had ruined everything.

"Be downstairs in five minutes," she said, storming out of the apartment. "Or not. I really don't care." Claire let the door slam behind her and trembled the entire elevator ride down. She fought back tears, waiting beside the cab. She wished she had been the one to abandon her family, not the one left behind to destroy it further. Julia made it down in time, but they did not speak again that morning.

•••••••••••••

Claire returned her focus to the present. The water had risen to her neck, forcing her to swim. From upstream, noise like a waterfall was growing at an alarming speed. Any more water and she was sure to drown. Panic set in as she realized she had lost track of how much further she needed to go.

Something large and sentient slid past her thigh, causing her to drop her phone. Unable to keep her face above water, she took a deep breath of rotten air and went under, letting the water pull her downstream. She swam frantically towards the dim rays of light just up ahead. The water pushed her quickly through the tunnel. By luck alone, her hand caught what she hoped was the steel rung of a ladder as the rushing water threatened to drag her away into the fetid black abyss beyond.

From under the septic water, she searched blindly for the next ladder rung. She was running out of air. She hadn't had enough time to catch a proper breath before the surging sewage overcame her. Her hand landed on the next hold, and then the next until, at last, she pulled herself free of the putrid river of waste. She drew in a large breath of humid air and dragged herself up towards the manhole cover. She braced her shoulders against the steel lid and pressed upward with all her remaining strength.

The lid barely shifted. She pressed one more time. Summoning a strength she had never known, she shifted the lid to the side. She climbed free of the sewers as quickly as her exhausted body would allow. She dared not look back at the city's annihilation. Besides, she only had eyes for the school before her.

Infested with pulsing veins and carpets of twitching skin, the school building stood tall and grotesque. It was now a monolith of flesh. No life stirred behind its shattered windows and missing doors. Claire wept as her broken and bloodied feet climbed the mucus-covered stairs. The last traces of the human race were slowly consumed by the devouring chaos in every direction. Above, the trumpeting shouts remained. Yet, she steeled herself against their horrific pull.

"Julia," Claire shouted upon entering the building. No reply. She moved further inside and tried again, but still nothing came. Julia had to be here; she knew it. She could feel it in her bones. Her daughter wouldn't have left without her. Claire's intuition drove her onward. She limped quickly across a tiled floor that had yet to be consumed by alien flesh.

"Mom," came a cry from the direction of the auditorium stairs.

"Julia," Claire's voice broke with hysterics. She climbed the stairs and burst through the sound room door. "Julia?"

"Momma," the small voice said, coming out from underneath a small table. Julia's face was wet with tears. "I didn't think you would come."

"Of course, I came," Claire said, pulling her daughter close. "You are my everything. No matter what, you've always been my everything."

No more words passed between them. They wept together as mother and child. Broken and bonded, doomed and pardoned. They were all each other would ever get and all they would ever need in this dying world. Claire could only smile as she gazed into Julia's eyes, as the school's walls were shorn apart by monstrous appendages of ravenous meat. She smiled, knowing that Julia was the most amazing miracle she had ever seen. Claire had created her, and for once, she had done something right.

OPEN DOOR

By Tom Paul

EVEN THOUGH SHE KNEW her mother had already locked all the doors and windows in their house, sixteen-year-old Ari checked them again. It was a chilly day in late September, getting dark, and this was no ordinary time for the once sleepy, middle-class neighborhood.

Over the last month, two high school girls went missing, leaving the entire town on edge. Their parents hadn't considered them a runaway risk. They disappeared two weeks apart and were not known to hang around together. With cell phones, purses, and all personal items left behind, they vanished into the night without a trace, leaving only an open front door.

Ari and her divorced mother lived in a modest brick home. She told her mother she was going upstairs to do her homework. In her bedroom, Ari sat down at her desk, took one look at her math book and grabbed her phone instead. Flopping down on her bed, she called her friend Pam, who lived on the same street.

In the same grade as Ari, Pam had moved into the leafy suburb the year before, with her mother, father, and older brother. The two girls quickly became friends. Though they attended the same school as the missing girls, neither knew them well.

"Hi, Ari," Pam said. "I'm glad you called. I'm getting tired of being a prisoner in my own house. My entire family is freaked out."

"Well, at least you've got your dad and brother there. It's only Mom and me over here. I just checked all the doors and windows again."

The girls went on talking until dark before resigning themselves to doing their homework.

After an hour, Ari noticed it had been unusually silent downstairs. She went to the top of the stairs and called, "Mom," but there was no reply. She tiptoed halfway down the stairs and called out again, but still no reply. Ari crept toward the bottom and peeked around the corner.

The front door was slightly ajar. She shouted, "Mom, where are you?" Footsteps inside the house came her way.

Heart racing, Ari ran back up the stairs and locked herself in the bathroom, the only upstairs room with a working lock. Then she remembered the phone was on her bed. She considered dashing out to retrieve it, but heavy footsteps and breathing continued up the staircase. The footsteps reached the top of the stairs, followed by a long silence.

Facing the door and trembling, Ari tried not to make a sound. The footsteps moved down the hallway in her direction. The heavy, ragged breathing stopped outside the bathroom door. She waited. Three harsh knocks drove her to the edge of passing out.

"Open up!" said the gruff male voice.

Ari stayed silent. The doorknob began moving back and forth, but the lock stayed firm. Three harder knocks followed.

"Go away!" she screamed.

The man's kick ripped the door open with such force the lock took part of the door frame with it. Ari saw the room swirl and passed out.

•••••••••••••

Five years later, the mystery of the town's three missing girls remained unsolved. Investigators found common circumstances in each incident: houses hidden from view, backdoors locked yet the front doors open, no sign of forced entry from the outside, only one adult present at the time, no recollection of unlocking or opening the front door, and most puzzling of all, no adult with any memory of what they were doing during the disappearance.

True crime writer, Trish Van der Meer, gathered up her belongings as she packed to make her final pre-publication trip to the small upstate New York town. At 36, the tough, trim ex-cop hoped her account of the missing girls would be her most successful book yet, and reignite interest in a case sorely lacking in forensic evidence.

Trish had proved her mettle as a cop, becoming a detective in only three years. A formidable martial arts practitioner, her combination of smarts and athleticism served her well. But it was her independent streak, that need to delve more deeply into the mechanics of crime that drove her out of police work and into writing.

Trish planned to re-interview all three of the victims' families one last time. Realistically, all she expected to find were additional details of the girls' lives to include in the book, but she knew her inner-cop would be on the lookout for any clue.

Trish also planned to check in with the local police, although she doubted she would be able to extract any new information from them. The town's small police force gave her a degree of grudging respect because of her law enforcement background, but they tended to treat her as a nuisance—*big-city cop looking down her nose at the local yokels.*

The final interview on her schedule, a last-minute arrangement, would be with one of the town's morticians, who claimed to have spent considerable time studying the case. She accepted the unusual request because, on occasion, she had received useful tips from eager-to-share-their-theories armchair detectives, but he had also made a comment about the possible perpetrator that she wanted to pursue.

••·•·••••·•·••

After the three-hour drive, Trish checked into her motel and prepared for her pre-arranged meetings with members of the three families. Their town always struck her as deceptively innocent, with its tree-lined streets, quaint little downtown, and river running through it. Sometimes, she thought it best for people not to look too deeply under the surface—they might not like what they see.

Fortunately, the families of the victims viewed her as a friend and ally. Ari's mother, who couldn't forgive herself for her lapse of vigilance at a time when the whole town was on high alert, was the most taxing to deal with. Trish noted the mother's tendency to drift off in the middle of a sentence, and wondered if her spaciness was part of the problem. All of the parents remained mystified at how their front doors became unlocked and why they had no memory of when the abductions were occurring.

The next morning, Trish visited the local police station and, as usual, they were less than eager to deal with her or share new information on the case. She suspected the chief, who insisted she deal only with him, was convinced she was out to portray the department as having bungled the investigation. *I've had about enough of his paranoid glare,* she told herself as she left the station. *Maybe I should have read him his rights before he spoke to me.* She walked out smiling.

This left the last interview, with the citizen sleuth mortician, scheduled for 3 p.m. at his home. Trish took the opportunity beforehand to go for a jog, shower back at her motel, and have lunch at a restaurant discovered on her previous trip.

Ten minutes ahead of her appointment time, Trish arrived at the mortician's residence, hidden by large trees at the end of a long driveway. She was grateful the residence was separate from his place of work. Observing the carefully manicured lawn and the well-maintained old Victorian house, she felt transported back in time—a time when appearances were more comforting, regardless of what lay underneath. The large wooden door featured an old-fashioned knocker in the shape of a placid-looking lion's head. Trish gave it three knocks and heard footsteps approaching.

"I'm Harold Baynes," said the large, mid-fortyish, ruddy-faced man who answered the door, smiling. "You must be Ms. Van der Meer."

"Yes, thank you for meeting with me," Trish said, as she shook his big, beefy hand. "Any light you can shed on this case would be truly appreciated."

"I'll do my best, and thank you for seeing me. Please come in and make yourself at home."

Harold led Trish into his well-appointed living room, where she sat in a comfortable chair near the fireplace. She glanced at the walls lined with relaxing, nineteenth-century-style landscapes, while Harold displayed the finely honed, gracious manner of someone in his profession.

"Can I bring you coffee, tea, or water?" he asked.

"Thank you, I'm fine," she replied.

Harold took a seat on his sofa.

"I'll try not to take up too much of your time," Trish said. "Do you mind if I record our conversation?"

"Of course not," he replied. "I've been investigating this case for years now, and will do anything I can to help. Where would you like me to begin?"

"In our brief conversation on the phone, you said you had insight into the type of person who might carry out these crimes. Especially how, at a time when the whole town was on high alert, the killer was able to get Ari's mother to unlock the door."

"Yes, that's correct," Harold said. "Let me start at the beginning. I had been discussing these cases with a fellow investigator when she brought up the possibility that the parents had been hypnotized beforehand to unconsciously respond to certain cues to unlock the doors. My thought was it just didn't seem very likely that anyone could have somehow been in the position to hypnotize all of them. Then I remembered something.

"Over twenty years ago, I met a man I'll call Steve. I should preface this by saying in no way am I suggesting he did these crimes, or any other crimes for that matter, since, to my knowledge, he's never even been in this part of the country. To just meet Steve, he seemed rather ordinary, but once I got to know him, he revealed he possessed some remarkable abilities. He claimed that by sheer force of will and concentration, he could telepathically impel an acquaintance to do simple things that they otherwise had no intention of doing, as long as they were unaware of what he was up to. For example, he could get a friend who was not even with him to come to him, and when they got there, they would have no idea why they were there."

"How did Steve discover he had this ability?" Trish asked.

"When he was a teenager, he found he could get his dog to do things just by mentally focusing on inserting it in the dog's mind. For example, without talking, he could transmit the idea of thirst, and the dog would go drink water from his bowl.

"He then tried his talents on his little sister. She'd end up doing things and have no awareness of why once she had done it. It was like she was in some kind of trance controlled by Steve. He found he could even induce a kind of stupor in her in which she'd get sleepy and go take a nap."

"So you think the kidnapper used these tactics to get to the girls?"

"I believe it would be possible." Harold paused and gazed at Trish, as if to judge if she was taking him seriously, and then continued. "He began expanding his scope. He'd go to places like a library to see if he could make a complete stranger inspect the magazine shelf. He found he had less success with people he didn't know. He concluded that as long as he was somewhat familiar with the person's mind, and they didn't know what he was up to, it had more chance of working."

As Harold spoke, Trish had a hunch it was very important to this large man's delicate ego that she pay close attention and respect his investigative instincts. She made an extra effort to appear to be taking him seriously. He continued to provide further examples of Steve's talents.

However, as Harold droned on, Trish was having difficulty following him. She became drowsy and fought to keep her eyes open. Alarmed, she looked back at Harold, who was sitting before her, taking it all in.

"Are you getting sleepy, Ms. Van der Meer?"

Trish struggled to rouse herself from her drowsiness. Although she was still conscious and could speak, she realized just how much strength had been draining out of her body, and her increasing alarm did not counteract it. She had lost control over her movements.

Harold watched her desperate attempts to rouse herself out of her stupor with amusement.

"Well, Ms. Van der Meer, I see you're one of the vulnerable ones. How unfortunate for you. When I took those three girls, I used the same technique on their protectors I'm now using on you. I have a talent for tuning into the brainwaves of certain individuals, and one thing I've found, past a certain point, once one vulnerable to my talents is in my grasp there's no escape, even if they realize what's going on. The more they struggle, the more I tighten my coils." Harold sat back and grinned. "You see, the more you struggle to escape my grasp, the more empowered I get! You look close to being totally helpless already, and I don't know how much longer I can resist putting my hands around your neck.

"People wonder why those particular girls were chosen. It was just a matter of vulnerability and geography. If I knew there was only one parent home at the time, and one I could control, if the house was secluded enough to permit me to operate in the way I needed, and if the daughter was attractive enough, they were candidates. Planning, you see. It's all in the planning."

In full panic mode, Trish struggled mightily to escape her stupor—nothing worked. She could barely move.

Harold grinned. "I meticulously studied the powers I could exert over those whose children I might prey upon. Yes, every one of the parents had been clients of mine over the years, giving me the opportunity I needed to see just how much I could control them. It was I who had taken care of their deceased relatives, just as it was I who later would seize control of their little minds, impelling them to mindlessly unlock and open their front door and remember nothing. They're simpletons, all of them. Once I had their little darlings, they were free to indulge their stupid grief and continue their insipid lives.

"You may be wondering why I'm choosing to target you. Do you have any idea how obnoxious it is for you, in all your arrogance, beauty, and privilege, to come waltzing into this little hamlet nosing around and hoping to make your mark as a true crime writer, no doubt indulging your fantasies of fame and glory? Well, you'll get your wish for fame, since you're about to become another true crime victim. Much to your credit, however, you did discover who the culprit was, in this, your last interview. That's more than anyone else did. Too bad you won't be around to capitalize on it. However, I will be adding you to my collection—quite an honor.

"Oh my!" Harold observed. "Is that a tear falling from your eye? You know, I don't know much about your background, but frankly, you impress me as someone who's had all the advantages from the get-go. What did I get in my life? Big ugly Harold, the weirdo mortician's son who couldn't get a date with a pretty girl to save his life. The die was cast from the time I was a teen, doomed to a life so miserable all I could ever hope for was to be just another mortician like my father. Every time I asked a pretty girl out when I was sixteen, they acted like it was a joke. I got rejected every time. They couldn't run away fast enough."

Trish struggled with all her might to break Harold's mental grip, but the more he prattled on about his resentments at the cards life had dealt him, the stronger his grip.

"The harder I tried to get what I wanted in life," Harold continued, "the more it was denied me. It was all a setup from the start. I couldn't win, so I finally came to a conclusion. After what I've had to put up with in life, I deserve some trophies to show for it. If I can't have what I want alive, I'll have them dead."

He glared triumphantly at the helpless Trish, who could see it all clearly. He wanted her to suffer, squeezing out of her all the smug arrogance he imagined she felt toward people like him—people she'd never give a second look to in ordinary life. His frustration and rage drove his focus. She experienced it as so powerful he might even be able to stop her from breathing, if he willed it.

Trish watched as Harold leaned back with a contemptuous half-grin, half-sneer, seemingly careful to maintain his focus but wishing to savor the suffering of his helpless prey. She saw the furious malice in his dark eyes, and faced a dreaded realization—*he really is going to strangle me!*

Three strong knocks on the front door startled Harold.

Alarmed, he looked around at the door and turned back to Trish. "Do you know who that is?"

"Yes."

"Well, who is it?"

"The cops."

"Why are they here?"

"Because."

"Because of what, goddammit!"

"Something you said," she replied, struggling to limber up and regain her strength, as Harold lost his focus.

"What did I say?"

"That you had a theory about how the killer got Ari's mother to unlock the door at a time the whole town was on high alert."

"So what the hell does that have to do with anything?" said Harold, sweating profusely.

"No investigator thought she'd unlock the door," Trish said, "especially since she had a peephole and bay window."

There were three harder knocks on Harold's door.

"If you don't get to the point, bitch, I'm going to take your head off!"

"When you called me, you spoke as if it were a fact she had unlocked the door. The police and everyone else had already concluded she didn't. If she really did, then only the abductor would know it, as well as how he got her to do it. If by any chance you were the abductor, I wanted to try to get you to implicate yourself before I had arranged for the police to arrive. Planning, you see. It's all in the planning."

Growling furiously, Harold charged Trish. He threw a ferocious right-handed punch at her head, striking a glancing blow as she ducked away to her right. She unleashed a kick to his groin, which partly missed its target, but slowed his charge. Harold struck another glancing blow to her face, but her less-than-full-force retaliatory kick hit the mark. Harold toppled, bent over, to the floor, and Trish delivered a kick to the head that left him laid out flat by the couch.

Trish turned, responding to the knocking and shouting outside. She shouted, "I'm unlocking the door!"

"Please come in," she said, breathing heavily as she opened the door. She could see by the cops' faces they were shocked at her appearance. She was bleeding from her nose and left ear, her hair was matted with blood, and her left eye was red and swelling.

"I'm afraid Harold has encountered a mishap," she said. "Those are his feet sticking out from behind the couch. He's bleeding and unconscious. You should call an ambulance. I recorded his confession. It's on the living room table."

The shell-shocked cops called for assistance. They began interrogating Trish, who insisted on staying at the scene as medics arrived and treated her. They listened to the recorded confession as Harold was whisked away to the hospital, handcuffed, and under armed guard.

Trish could feel the tension as more police and investigators converged on the scene and disappeared into the hallways and rooms of Harold's lair. After five years, there was now a real possibility of discovering the girls' fate. She watched as one of the officers opened the door to the locked basement with a crowbar. A feeling of dread overcame her as she heard him going downward.

As Trish would later recount in her book, "He walked down the basement stairs and wedged open the bottom door. After five long years, the three girls were finally found—sitting on chairs arranged in a semicircle, wearing the clothes they had disappeared in, and silently facing the throne of the lord of the manor—all three embalmed by the meticulous hands of mortician Harold Baynes."

YOU NEED TO COME IN HERE

By C. R. Langille

DAVE TAPPED ON THE steering wheel of the old Toyota Tacoma, following the beat of Beastie Boys' "Sabotage." He couldn't help nodding his head along with it as well. His dad had played it for him when he was just a little tyke, and it must have created a connection deep in his subconscious because whenever it came on, he would always let it play in its entirety, even though it reminded him of his jackass dad.

Greta reached over to switch it, but Dave playfully slapped their hand away. "What? Are you crazy?"

They rolled their eyes, smiling, sending Dave back to the first time he ran into them at the local coffee shop. He was leaving just as they were coming in, and they shared a brief moment. They smiled, and it was all over. Dave came back to the coffee shop each day at the same time until he ran into them again. The rest was history.

"I think you're the crazy one, my love. This is sabotage," he sang in time with the song.

Greta giggled before looking out the window.

"Check it out. We're hitting a different microsystem or something. The trees are starting to change a bit. Not just sage and juniper," Greta said.

Aspen lined either side of the road in a twisting maze and tangle. Dave remembered reading somewhere that the trees were all connected to the same system or something like that. One organism. Or were those mushrooms that did that? He couldn't remember for sure. Maybe both.

A weathered sign let them know there was a gas station up ahead, and it was the last service for the next 80 miles. He glanced at the gas gauge—half full. They could probably make it just fine, but he wanted to play it safe. Plus, he had to piss something fierce.

"I'm going to stop up here. We can fill up and get some snacks or something before we get to the trailhead," Dave said.

"Oh yeah. I hope they have those caramel M&Ms. Those are the absolute best!"

The road curved, and when they came around, the fill station came into view. It was literally a wooden shack with an old gas pump out front that would have needed replacing back in the 50s. The place looked condemned, but there was an open sign in the window and an old Chevy pickup parked out front.

"I just hope they take credit cards," Dave said. He debated just driving past and dealing with it, but he didn't want to seem like a wuss to Greta, and the urge to pee was getting worse by the second.

He pulled the truck in next to the gas pump and hopped out. Filling up could wait because he had to hit the restroom first. As he half-jogged over to the building, he spied a sticker in the window saying they took Visa, Mastercard, and American Express, and he sighed in relief.

Dave walked through the door with Greta right behind him. The motion set a small cowbell ringing, which caught the attention of an older woman sitting behind the desk reading a magazine. She looked up at the pair with a toothless grin that turned sour as soon as she spied Greta.

“Excuse me, where are your restrooms?” Dave asked.

The woman wouldn’t take her eyes off Greta, and Dave could feel the tension rising. Greta got closer to Dave, hugging their own torso.

“Ma’am?” Dave asked, raising his voice.

The woman snapped her gaze from Greta to Dave, then motioned toward the back. “Back there. But don’t use the urinal. It’s broken,” she said, once again eyeing Greta.

Dave and Greta sauntered off in the direction the woman pointed. Near the back of the store was a tiny hallway that led to a single bathroom.

“What was that about?” Greta asked.

“Small town crap, I guess. You okay?”

Greta forced a smile and nodded. “Yeah, not the first time. Probably won’t be the last time.”

“How about you go first? I’ll wait just in case.”

“In case what, the old woman wants to come in and make sure I’m not using the urinal? I’ll be fine. Go ahead.”

“You sure?” Dave asked

“Go! Your eyes are turning yellow,” Greta said with a chuckle.

Dave opened the door and was immediately assaulted by the smell of piss and mildew. The toilet was missing the lid, and the rim was covered in tiny hairs and caked with dried urine.

"Nice," he muttered under his breath.

He went as quick as he could and cleaned up the toilet to the best of his ability so Greta wouldn't have to deal with the old mess (points for not throwing up during the process). After, Dave washed his hands extra clean but had to dry them on his pant legs because the only thing in the restroom was one of those old-timey rolling cloth units. However, this one hadn't been serviced in a long time due to the tan stains on the towel. There was just no way he was going to touch that thing.

Dave stepped out and expected to see Greta waiting for their turn. He planned on warning them that the restroom needed to be burned to the ground, but they weren't there.

His heart skipped a beat, and he quickly looked around the store but couldn't find them. He started to walk to the door, but the woman behind the counter chirped up, still sporting that toothless grin.

"Where y'all headed?"

Dave peered out the dirty window, hoping to see Greta by the truck. But again, they weren't there.

"Uh... a cave," he answered absentmindedly. He looked all around, still unable to find Greta. Worry began to settle in his stomach.

"Oh, y'all going to Mammoth Cave? I think you're headed in the wrong direction."

Dave pulled his cell phone out of his pocket, hoping to find a message from Greta, but there wasn't any service.

"What? Oh, no, we're going to a different cave. I think it's called Heart Cave or something. Hey, did you see where my spouse went?"

The woman's smile dropped. She spat a wad of tobacco out into a no-shit bronze spittoon before answering. "You'll want to stay away from that place. It's dangerous."

"Don't worry, we're experienced spelunkers. But you didn't answer my question. Where did Greta go?"

It was a lie. They were amateur at best. But how dangerous could it be? It wasn't like they were going to go crawling through tiny tubes and get stuck or something.

"I don't know where your pretty-looking boyfriend went. Somewhere outside. Maybe to hug a tree or something."

Dave's face flushed with heat. Greta wasn't Dave's boyfriend because they weren't a man. They were non-binary. He thought about making a stink about it, but it wasn't worth the energy to get into it with some rando in a gas station that he'd probably never see again. He dug into his wallet, produced a $20 bill, and threw it on the counter. "For the gas."

As he stormed out, the woman behind the counter said, "Stay away from that place, you hear? It ain't safe!"

Dave walked around the building, calling out for Greta. He found them staring at the exterior wall of the gas station.

"Jesus Christ, there you are," Dave said. He rushed over to Greta and pulled them into a tight embrace.

Greta jumped at the touch but smiled when they saw him. "Oh, hey. We ready?"

"Not yet, gotta fill up the truck. Be careful of the bathroom. It's a crime scene."

"I couldn't wait, so I came out here and went in the woods. But on the way back, I found this."

Greta pointed to the wall, and Dave saw what they had been looking at.

"What in the...?"

Fastened to the wall with screws, nails, and old rusty wire was a collage of animal bones blasted white by the elements. They formed a spiral pattern with a huge bull elk skull in the center.

"What is this?" Dave asked, still unsure of what he was looking at.

"I don't know, but it's kind of beautiful."

Dave pulled his gaze away from the bone art to look at Greta in disbelief. "You can't be serious. This is messed up."

They both stared at it for another moment before Dave pulled Greta away and headed back to the truck.

The gas station attendant watched them from the window with a grim expression. This whole place gave Dave the creeps, and he wanted to get the heck out of there and to the cave as soon as possible.

"Let's go," Dave said.

"Yeah. Good idea."

Dave put $20 worth of gas into the truck, and they sped down the road.

•••·•·••••·••·•••

Two hours later, after a long stretch of road that zig-zagged through the wilderness (Dave had started thinking it was an ATV trail and not meant for trucks due to the rugged terrain), they pulled up to the trailhead. By this time, the gas station attendant was nothing more than a toxic memory that would boil over in his thoughts every now and then. However, Dave couldn't stop thinking about that bone spiral.

"What do you think it meant?" he asked.

Greta rubbed her temples. "What?"

"The bones? What do you think they meant?"

Greta dug around in their backpack before pulling out a bottle of painkillers. They popped the top, threw two little red pills into their mouth, and washed them down with a lukewarm soda that had gone flat from all the bumps on the road.

"I don't know. It was weird, but kind of pretty."

"You okay?" Dave asked.

"Yeah, I just have a killer headache. Probably dehydrated."

"Hydrate or di—"

Greta held up a finger to silence him. "Don't you dare say it."

Dave laughed and put his hands up in defeat. He killed the truck and stepped out, admiring the wilderness surrounding them. Pines and aspens stood sentry on either side of the trail. Up above, ravens croaked to one another.

The clink of the engine cooling was foreign in a place like this, and Dave couldn't wait to get down the trail and away from any semblance of civilization. So they gathered their daypacks, ensured they had enough water and some food, then set off toward the trailhead.

Greta stopped at the trees and traced their finger along the spiral. "Weird."

Dave was digging through his pack to find the GPS. "What's weird?"

"Look at this."

The trailhead was a cut path through several aspens. Someone a long time ago had marked both trees with a spiral—a spiral that reminded him of the gas station wall.

"No way," he said under his breath.

"Do you think we should turn back around and go somewhere else? A jacuzzi tub at a hotel sounds kind of nice."

Dave mulled it over. They had driven a long way to get to this exact spot, and according to his research, the cave was supposed to be quite spectacular.

"I think we'll be fine. Maybe it's just a coincidence," Dave said. He didn't believe it entirely, but a small part of his brain screamed at him to get back in the truck and drive back to town as fast as possible. However, there was the curious part of him that wanted to push on. "Come on, if it gets weird, we'll turn around and find that jacuzzi."

Greta gave him a half-smile and nodded. He could tell they weren't 100% sold on the idea, but they were at least willing to give it a go. That's what he loved about them—their sense of adventure and excitement.

Dave turned the GPS on, marked the location of the truck, and they set off into the woods. As they hiked along the path, every so often, they would find another aspen tree with a spiral like a strange trail blaze.

All around them, the woods were full of life. Squirrels chattered away, sometimes screaming at them from above. Birds chirped and flew overhead. And to top it all off, the sun was warm, and a slight breeze made the temperature damn near perfect.

After a while, Dave looked at the GPS to see how far they had gone. He figured maybe they had hiked a couple of miles, which meant they would be close to the cave. However, when he looked at the device, it said it was searching for a signal. Their marker hadn't updated since the truck.

"Crap," he said.

"What is it?"

"The GPS isn't working."

Greta's eyes went wide. "What does that mean? Are we lost?"

Dave looked up and found another spiral blaze. He looked behind them and could see a few markers on the backsides of the trees. "No, we can follow the path back out easily enough."

"We've officially hit the 'getting weird' portion."

Dave looked at Greta and could see the fear in their eyes. He stared down the path, full of quaking aspens, quivering with anticipation. He imagined the trees were curious as to what the pair would do. But he had made a promise.

"Okay."

Greta let out a sigh of relief and hugged him. "Thank you."

"Of course. I wouldn't want to get lost out here. Nobody would find us. Hiking in the woods at night is a recipe for disaster. Without the GPS, it would be too easy to get turned around."

He was bummed, but he fully believed the truth in his own words. One miscalculation and they could start hiking off-course. After a quick pee break, they turned around and headed back to the trailhead.

After nearly 30 minutes, Dave stopped and looked around. He pulled the GPS out of his pocket and checked it, hoping there would be a signal this time. However, it still couldn't connect to the satellites.

"What's up?" Greta asked.

"Well, when we started hiking, we were heading downhill."

"Okay, and?" Greta folded their arms across their chest and peered through the trees.

"Well, we turned around to head back, but we're still heading downhill. It doesn't make sense."

"Maybe it's just your mind playing tricks, or maybe we got turned around somewhere?"

"No way. We started heading south from the truck. By all accounts, we should be heading north. But look up in the sky where the sun is. We're still heading south."

Greta saddled up close to Dave, and he put an arm around them. It didn't add up.

"I'm going to climb that tree over there," Dave said, pointing to an old pine. "Maybe I can get high enough to get a signal."

Deep down, he didn't think it would work, but on the off chance that it did, he could at least get their bearing and figure out which direction they had to go to get back to the truck.

"Seems sketchy," Greta said.

"Look, we don't have much time before it gets dark. Maybe four hours or so. I don't want to spend the night out here if we can help it."

Greta grabbed him by the cheeks and kissed him. "Be careful."

"I always am."

They chuckled. "Liar."

Dave dropped his pack and jogged over to the tree. He devised a plan to climb up, choosing the strongest-looking branches, and headed up. When he was a kid, this would have been easy. But now, fear, doubt, and aching muscles harassed him with every movement. Finally, he got high enough that he decided to give it a try.

Dave pulled the GPS out of his pocket, turned it on, and waited. He stared at the tiny screen as it told him it was searching for a signal.

"Come on...."

"Anything?" Greta shouted from below.

"No, not ye—"

The woods went silent all around him. It was like something had flipped a switch and turned on noise-canceling headphones. Dave broke out in a cold sweat, and his leg started to tremble. He had the uncanny sense that something was watching him. Not just Greta from below, but *something* else. Then, just like that, the sound of the wilderness returned along with the beep of the GPS.

It connected. Dave's heart soared as he saw the map load up. It still showed their last known position, which was the truck at the trailhead.

"It's working!"

Any moment now, it would update and show their current location. However, all those thoughts melted away as the branch underneath his foot cracked. Dave reached out as he went weightless and fell before hitting another branch beneath him. The wood scraped up his leg, digging into his skin. He grabbed onto a nearby branch to stop himself from falling even further, but by doing so, the GPS slipped out of his hand and fell.

He groaned, holding on as tight as he could for what felt like forever.

"I'm okay," Dave said, more to himself than for Greta.

That's when he realized Greta hadn't said anything during his fall.

"Greta! You okay?"

Visions of them lying on the dirt, brained by a falling branch, filled his imagination. He looked around, hoping he wouldn't find them sprawled out underneath. However, Greta wasn't anywhere to be found.

"Greta! Where are you?"

Anger replaced fear. Why the hell would they wander away while he was risking life and limb to climb a janky tree?

"Greta!"

No answer.

He grumbled and started his slow descent, careful where he placed his feet as he didn't want to hazard another fall. Unfortunately, he didn't find Greta when he got to the bottom. He did find their backpack, though.

"Greta! Where are you?"

Again, there was no answer. Dave started to walk over to where the GPS was, but stopped after the first step when pain lanced up his leg. Dave hobbled over to a nearby rock and sat down, pulling his pant leg up. His leg had a nasty gash where the branch had scraped him. It might need stitches, but at the moment, he needed to clean the wound and bandage it up.

Dave grabbed his pack, fished out the first aid kit, and did his best with what he had. It wasn't great, but it was better than nothing. Then, he limped over to the GPS. Hopefully, the device had updated before the fall, but his heart dropped to his knees when he picked it up.

The screen was cracked, as it had landed on a rock and wouldn't turn on.

He let out a string of expletives that would have made a Marine blush. Dave looked all around, hoping to find Greta; however, there wasn't any sign of them.

"Greta! This isn't funny! Where are you?"

At first, there was nothing. But then the wind picked up and brought their voice to him.

"Help!"

"Where are you? What's wrong?"

Dave's heart went into overdrive. He moved as fast as he could following their voice, his leg be damned.

"Help! You need to come in here!"

"Where?" Dave screamed.

He moved toward the voice, which was further down the trail. His leg throbbed with each step, but he pushed through the pain. Eventually, the path led him to a rocky hillside with a dark cave opening.

The cave. The place they had been hiking to before everything went south. It looked nondescript enough except for the spiral petroglyph carved into a sandy-colored boulder sitting at the mouth.

"Greta?" He limped closer to the entrance. "Are you in there?"

Their voice came from the darkness further inside. "Help! You need to come in here!"

A thousand questions raced through Dave's mind. Why had they gone wandering off alone while he was in the tree? Why in the hell did they go into the cave when they were already spooked? It didn't add up. However, it didn't matter either. They needed help, and he was the only one who could provide that help. He dug his headlamp out of his pack and entered the cave.

The temperature dropped immediately, and the smell of water and dirt attacked his nose. The mouth was fairly wide, but his light showed the tunnel narrowed quickly.

"Greta? Are you hurt?"

"Help!"

Their voice bounced off the cave wall, seemingly coming from all directions, but logically, they had to be deeper down the tunnel.

"I'm coming!"

Dave moved as fast as he could. As he did, his headlamp illuminated more petroglyphs along the walls. Spirals. Giant serpent-like squiggles. People, or things that looked like people, lined up in front of the giant squiggles. There was something about the shapes that made the hair on his arms stand straight. The whole vibe of the cave was off, and he wanted to get out of there as soon as possible.

The ceiling started to get lower and lower the further he went until he was on his hands and knees.

No way had Greta come this far. They were too smart to venture off alone, and he knew they would have never in a million years been caught crawling in a cave tunnel.

"Greta! Where are you?"

"Help! You need to come in here!"

Again, their voice came from all around him. However, this time it was louder, which meant he was getting closer.

Dave crawled further down the tunnel as it continued to get even narrower. He wasn't scared of tight places, but this was something else. He didn't like how the rock's edges grabbed at his shirt or caught his shoes. The breeze coming up the tunnel was warm, and... was it rancid?

Dave crawled even further, losing track of time. Soon, the rock walls brushed his shoulders as sweat poured down his face, stinging his eyes. As he crawled, the tunnel narrowed, getting tighter and smaller until it surrounded him. He wasn't claustrophobic, but there was something about this tunnel that crawled under his skin. Dave labored for air, and the tight rock walls squeezing him didn't make it any easier. He hoped that there would be a place to turn around up ahead, because crawling out backward, unable to see, didn't appeal to him.

Finally, his light came across Greta. They were ahead in the tunnel right in front of him. He couldn't see much but the soles of their boots, but he recognized the rainbow laces.

"Greta! Thank god! We need to get out of here."

They didn't answer. Dave crawled up as close as he could, which wasn't far enough. Greta's feet were ahead, but the tunnel narrowed even further. There was no way in hell he'd fit in there, and he was surprised that Greta got that far.

"Greta?"

They didn't answer. Dave tried to shimmy forward but only managed to gain a couple of inches. He stretched his arm out, his fingertips just brushing the back of their boot. As he did, the cave grumbled.

It was the best way to describe it. Perhaps it was an earthquake, or rocks shifting, but regardless, Dave wanted to get them the hell out of the cave and back under the open sky. He swore the tunnel tightened around him, even though he wasn't moving. Dave tried to ignore the sensation by keeping his breathing steady, but failed miserably. He was going to hyperventilate soon. He reached out one more time, stretching as far as he could. This time, he grabbed the heel of Greta's boot and gave it a little shake.

"Come on, let's get the heck out of here," Dave said.

Again, no answer. He shook their boot even harder, causing their leg to flip 180 degrees.

The leg ended at the knee, revealing bone and gristle. It was covered in dirt and ragged, as if something had been chewing on it.

Dave pulled his hand back as if the leg were a viper ready to strike. He wanted to scream, but the tunnel had closed in on him, squeezing the air from his lungs. Dave tried shuffling backward, but his pants caught on the ragged rock, trapping him.

Tears ran down his face as he tried to figure out what to do.

"Help! You need to come in here!"

Greta's voice came from the darkness in front of him. He looked up, and a pair of eyes reflected the light of his headlamp back at him.

Dave breathlessly tried to escape, but the cave tunnel was too narrow. The rocks bit and tore at his exposed skin, and no matter how hard he contorted his body, there was no way out.

"Help! You need to come in here!"

This time, it didn't sound like Greta. This time, it was raspy, tinny, and sounded like dozens of voices talking in unison.

Another blast of hot air hit Dave in the face, and his headlamp went dark. He scrambled to get it turned on again until finally, through some miracle, the light came back to life. Greta stared at him with a wide grin and teeth that were too long.

Dave screamed just as something grabbed his foot.

•••••••••••••

Hank Thomas and his subordinate, Rudy, from the Garfield County Search and Rescue, walked down the trail. Hank lit a cigarette and looked at one of the spirals carved into the aspen trees.

"Who do you think did this?"

Rudy shrugged. "No clue. Not the Forest Service, though, their blazes look different."

"Fact."

"What was up with that crazy old lady at the gas station? I mean, straight out of a horror movie, am I right?" Rudy asked.

"You got that right. So you think we'll find these two?"

"Who knows? I mean, that was their truck up at the trailhead. My guess is we'll find something."

The pair continued walking until they found a backpack on the ground. Rudy dug through it and found a worn canvas wallet with a dabbing unicorn on the front. After a quick inspection, he looked up at Hank.

"Well, you going to say something or just leave me hanging here?" Hank asked.

"It's one of theirs."

Hank nodded. He expected to find them, but it had been almost a week since they were supposed to be back home, so his hopes of finding them alive weren't too high.

Hank was about to say they should press on when the forest around them fell silent. It was only for a moment, but it gave him the heebie-jeebies. He'd be happy when they were back at the office, as there was something about this forest he didn't like. Then, as fast as it had happened, the wilderness sounds came back to life, and a breeze came from down the trail.

"Help! You need to come in here!"

It was a man's voice. The pair stopped what they were doing, looked at one another, and then headed toward the voice.

"This is Search and Rescue! Are you hurt?"

The pair continued going down the trail until they reached a cave entrance.

Rudy cupped his hands and yelled into the mouth of the cavern. "Anyone down there?"

"Help! You need to come in here!"

Hank radioed back to let the others know what was happening, but all he got back was static. Hank and Rudy looked at one another and then plunged into the cave.

DON'T TAKE THE STAIRS

By Nidheesh Samant ~ "This one goes out to all my loved ones who continue supporting my endeavours."

NISHA GOT OUT OF the cab and rushed onto the street. Moving as fast as her stilettos and pencil skirt allowed her to, she read the plaques at the entrance of each building. She spotted her destination near the end of the street. *Centenary Rose*. Nisha sighed. The building, living up to its name, looked like a hundred-year-old withered flower. Nisha paused, considering her decision to interview here. She shook her head. She was in no position to give up an opportunity for aesthetic reasons. She pushed open the gate and let herself in.

Before stepping into the lobby, she caught her reflection in the mirror at the entrance. She adjusted her auburn hair, white blouse, and black skirt. She practiced her confident smile, mentally assuring herself that this job was hers for the taking.

Some buildings, especially in the industrial sector, had the peculiar characteristic of having wretched exteriors but elegant interiors. Nisha had seen it before. However, this was not one of those buildings. The lobby looked squalid, with wallpaper barely sticking on the walls and only specks of grey tiles remaining on the concrete floor. Nisha carefully made her way through her poorly lit surroundings. The musty smell immediately drew a series of sneezes from her.

"Bless you."

Nisha gasped and turned in the direction of the speaker. An old security guard hobbled towards her. He looked almost as old as this building. To Nisha's surprise, even his hunched frame towered over her.

"Sir, I'm here for an interview. I wasn't told which floor to go to."

The gaunt-faced man gave her a grin. Nisha noticed most of his teeth were missing. The old man held out five bony fingers and pointed in the direction of a narrow passage. The flickering sign on the wall indicated it was the way to the lift and stairs.

"Thank you, sir. I must hurry. Good day to you."

Nisha rushed off without waiting for a reply. As soon as she had taken a couple of steps towards the passageway, she felt an ice-cold grip on her shoulder. It was the old man.

"Dear lady, take the lift. Don't take the stairs. The stairs take an eternity."

He flashed a rictus grin before letting Nisha go. She nodded and hurried away from the creepy security guard. He stood in his spot, watching her enter the passageway.

The passageway was an extension of the lobby. Dimly lit, it smelled of mold and decay. Nisha pressed the button for the lift and waited, gently massaging her shoulder. The area where the old man had clasped her felt oddly frozen and rigid. The lift indicator read "5" when Nisha pushed the button. The number showed no signs of changing. Nisha checked her watch. Only five minutes left. She pressed the button again and again, aware that it wasn't going to speed the machine up, but she didn't know what else to do.

Four minutes to go, and the lift hadn't moved. She looked at the stairs. There was no other choice. Climbing five floors in four minutes was doable. Yes, her feet would protest for the next couple of days, but the pain would be worth it if she landed the job. Nisha punched the button one last time. The red number refused to change. She threw her hands in the air and walked over to the stairwell.

The entrance door creaked open with a push. Nisha entered cautiously. However, the stairwell amazed her. It bore a stark contrast to the rest of the building. The area was well lit, the walls freshly painted, and the stairs perfectly waxed. The door swung shut behind her as Nisha began her five-floor ascent. Her stilettos clacked on each step as she climbed. The first flight took no effort. Nisha checked her watch. Three minutes to go. She pumped herself up as she climbed up the second flight. She could only marvel at how symmetrical and perfect the stairwell looked. Every floor looked exactly the same. She pushed herself to climb another flight without a break. Three floors done.

Nisha was now feeling the burn in her lungs and legs. She paused to rest and check her watch. It still showed three minutes to go. That couldn't be right. For a second, she considered the possibility that her watch had stopped working. However, she could see the second hand move. She brought the watch close to her ear. Sure enough, she could hear the ticking as well. Perhaps she was faster than she gave herself credit for.

As she climbed the fourth flight of stairs, she noticed a scratch on the wall. A speckle of green on an otherwise immaculate ivory. She ignored it and trooped on. Her breaths grew slightly heavier by the time the fourth flight was finished. Her watch still showed that three minutes remained. Nisha was now convinced that her watch was broken. She shook her head and focused on her goal. Just one flight to go. She spotted the green speck on the wall again, in the same location as the previous floor. This one was slightly larger.

Nisha was breathing through her mouth by the time she reached the door to exit to the fifth floor. She clutched the handle and pushed. It didn't budge. She tried with more force, and still there was no give. Nisha puffed and tried the handle with both hands. And again, it stood rooted in place. Nisha felt the onset of panic. She banged the metal door with her fists.

"Hello there! Could someone please open up? This door seems locked."

There was no response. Nisha began walking down the stairwell. She would try the exit door on the fourth floor. As she went down, she noticed the green speckle again. However, this time, it was more of a splash. Could it have spread further, somehow? She tried to pay it no heed and focused on the next door. Even this one wouldn't budge. Nisha was now sweating, her heart palpitating with fear. She did not care about being late anymore. She just wanted to get out of this staircase.

Nisha descended towards the ground floor, counting down the floors in her mind. *Three*. The splash of green had covered half of the wall, its wiry tendrils spreading in every direction like a network of veins. *Two*. Almost the entire wall was covered in green now. *One*. Even the ceiling was showing flecks of the same sick shade. *Zero*.

Nisha had arrived. Or so she thought. Strangely, the flight of stairs went further down. Coughing and gasping for air, she second-guessed her count. She descended another floor and saw that there was yet another flight of stairs. Nisha's eyes welled up. She tried the handle on this door. And yet again, it wouldn't open.

She screamed in desperation. The green had spread to the entire ceiling now, threatening to swallow Nisha next. While she sobbed, her mind running out of options, she heard footsteps coming from the floor below.

"Hey! Could you please help me? I am trapped here. Please get me out."

The footsteps only quickened in response. A mix of terror and anticipation left her unable to move. A head popped out from the turn of the stairs. She realized it was the old security guard. He shot Nisha his rictus grin as he spotted her. Although her vision was blurred due to tears, something was off about him. His gaunt skin was now covered in sickly speckles of green.

"Dear lady, why did you take the stairs? I warned you."

Her shoulder went numb again. Nisha wailed in horror. She scrambled up the stairwell, trying to put as much distance between herself and the old man as she could. Huffing and wheezing, she ascended floor after floor. The echoing sound of the old man's footsteps continued after her.

Nisha felt bile build up in her throat, threatening to spew out any second. Her legs trembled. She didn't know how long she could keep it up.

Suddenly, she heard a sharp snap and fell face-first onto the floor. Her right stiletto's heel had broken. Nisha blacked out for a second before waking up in agony. She pushed herself off the ground and felt a searing pain shoot up her right leg, forcing her to sit down again. Her ankle had swollen up. Nisha took deep breaths. She couldn't take it anymore. She got up from her position and limped to the exit door next to her. She made a last-ditch attempt at the handle.

To her surprise, the handle turned. She ecstatically pulled open the door, only to find the area walled in with bricks. A thick, green gelatinous layer oozed out from between the bricks, covering up the wall in no time. Nisha spotted her reflection in the grime—her face had turned as gaunt as the security guard's. Her eyes had sunken in, and patches of skin had disappeared completely, leaving her skeleton exposed. Her few tufts of remaining hair had turned white. She backed away in absolute horror and felt her face. She could feel more rough bones than skin. Nisha collapsed to her knees, surrendering to her surroundings. The security guard had been right.

The stairs took an eternity.

A CROOKED CANE COMES KNOCKING

By Winston Malone ~ "For Mom. Thank you for watching scary movies with me."

A MUTED THUD CAME from the doorway leading to the other side—the beckoning knock that had become impossible to ignore. Thomas Traylor rubbed a rough hand through his beard, stood from the side of his bed, and got dressed. He grabbed his Glock 19 and holstered it under his jacket. Access to the other side wasn't new to him; it was a part of his life now, whether he liked it or not.

Thomas approached the ethereal gate that more often than not functioned as his standing mirror. The darkness within it was a truer reflection of the real world than he liked to admit. He wasn't usually pessimistic, but sometimes he had to face the facts, and life was Hell. Even so, to overcome one's fears, one must face them. And that's what he planned to do: face *them.*

Thomas briefly touched the crucifix hanging at his neck before tucking the necklace under his shirt. He stepped into the scarlet-bordered, rippling rectangle, leaving his one-bedroom Nashville apartment to enter a realm of entropy, mimicry, and death. The liquid mirror chilled his skin, moving over clothing like a watery film. Thankfully, the strange substance, if he could call it that, left no residue as he passed through.

On the other side, massive spikes jutted from the ground like an ancient, fiendish forest, surrounding him in all directions. These spikes resembled dying trees, their branches nothing but jagged tendrils moving ever so slightly, reaching out to him. Pleading. Overhead, a reddish-black sky loomed, and the longer he stared into it, the darker it seemed to become, as if light had no place here, much like him.

Nearby, Thomas discovered a dilapidated trailer home, or rather, an imitation of one—the proportions slightly off. He recognized the faults in the roof's angles, the off-colored siding, and the uneven window frames. Whatever this reality was, it had never been able to truly copy his own, despite its apparent desire to do so.

"Help me, Mister," a raspy female voice said from the direction of the house.

Thomas Traylor stepped closer, searching for who had called out. Squinting, he made out a dark shape in the crawl space where the protective wall beneath the trailer home had broken. The shape shifted in the shadows, a mass of black hair and even blacker eyes.

"Mister, I'm so glad you came. Please come closer," the airy, girlish voice said. "I know the way to what you seek, what you desire, what you need to end your search. But you must help me first."

He didn't answer. He wasn't certain he could, even if he wanted to.

"You must decide quickly. They are coming."

There was a spine-tingling crack in the distance. Thomas twisted to see the men—no, the creatures shaped like men—coming out of the spiked woods in a loping run. They would kill him if they discovered him.

"Come in here, Mister. I'll show you the way."

Thomas stared at the shimmering, portal-like eyes of the shape within the crawl space—an obsidian grin spreading wide in that inky canvas. The shape backed away from the opening, an invitation to his escape, to his survival.

Gritting his teeth, Thomas knelt and entered the cramped maw. It swallowed him wholly to deposit him into the underbelly of the underworld, the void between, a place not even the creatures shaped like men could reach.

•••••••••••••

Abigail Rivers choked on the cigarette between her fingers. Coughing, phlegm broke apart in her throat. She'd caught something at work but hadn't been able to shake it for weeks.

On her porch, she watched the sun dip behind the northern Tennessee tree line. Warm breath puffed from her lips in a cloud that coalesced with the smoke exiting her lungs. Despite bundling in her favorite long-sleeve, faded blue jeans, and puffy black jacket, she felt winter's icy chill crowd her. It always found her. The warmth from her childhood cut like a second umbilical the day her mother died.

Abigail stamped the cigarette butt into an ashtray perched on the thin porch railing. Strange thumps had kept her awake all morning. She hated working the night shift—all the sounds of waking life proving how inconsiderate the world was for anything or anyone going against the grain.

She opened the glass door to lean into the living room. "Hey, Rick—" The box-shaped twenty-something raised his eyebrows in acknowledgement as he rocked out of the recliner to head to the kitchen. "—you hear anything odd around the house lately?"

Ricky opened the fridge. ESPN highlights of a Tennessee Titans game played on the TV, the announcers' voices droning on in that irritating tone that soaked up every bit of silence in the house. It blared at a volume just a decimal too high. *Always.*

Ricky closed the fridge and trudged back into the living room. "Lately? I mean, the air conditioner needs looking at, but that's been for a while." He cracked open the beer can and took a long chug as he sat back down.

"Okay. Well, I couldn't sleep because of something bumping around under the house or in the walls. It's probably mice again."

He grunted, focusing more on the TV than her.

"I have to head to work. I guess I'll see you later." The door started to swing shut.

"Wait, did I do something wrong?"

Abigail held the door ajar, indicating that she did not want to have a whole conversation. "No, no. It's fine. Just in my head a lot right now... you know."

"Oh, crap. I'm so sorry. I forgot about—"

"Don't worry, Rick. It's nothing I haven't handled every year already. I'll see you in the morning, okay?"

"Have a good shift, babe," he said, leaning back in the recliner and slurping the beer.

Abigail let the door drift shut. Glancing back to make sure it closed, something caught her eye. The reflection in the glass had distorted, creating some sort of optical illusion, but as it shut and remained still, it was not a mistake on her part. The man in the chair was not Ricky. He was elderly. He grinned at her as he leaned forward, his rotten teeth visible, his wispy, grey hair sprouting out at the sides.

Abigail tripped backward on the welcome mat. She caught herself, but her elbow knocked the ashtray off the railing. The small glass bowl shattered against a cinder block down below. She cursed, then looked back at the old man. He was gone. Ricky sat up as far as he could in the recliner, his feet still kicked out.

"You all right, babe?" he yelled through the door.

Abigail waved it off. She didn't want to interact with her boyfriend any more than she had to tonight. She loved him, but that love had faded into something more akin to that of a brother or friend; the passion pushed aside with every blaring football game, every beer, every ill-timed prank that only served to upset her.

Her Converse crunched the thin layer of snow that had settled on the stairs and the short sidewalk to the driveway. She got into her '96 Plymouth Turismo and started the ignition. Her windshield had a thin layer of ice, so she cranked up the defrost and lit another cigarette while she waited for it to melt.

Abigail blew smoke out of the window; despite the chill, she couldn't handle the cramped confines of the vehicle most days. The cold was with her whether she liked it or not, so the window was at least something she had control over.

After the wipers removed the moisture clinging to the windshield, Abigail reversed out of the driveway and drove to the next place she wouldn't be able to escape.

••·•·••••·•·•••

The cigarette pack sat upright in the cup holder, glistening under each passing streetlight, the gold-etched foil rising from the bottom to the top in iconic Cane's brand fashion. Abigail had smoked it ever since she could get her hands on them, the same brand her mother liked for all the wrong reasons.

Knock.

Abigail jumped in her seat and swerved a little at the sudden noise. It was the same thump she'd heard in the house. She looked around but saw nothing. It reverberated from nowhere and everywhere all at once, faint but definitely not her imagination.

Knock.

She coughed. Her throat burned. The intensity was much worse than before, and the thumping grew louder.

Knock.

An overwhelming desire filled her veins. It ached for the flickering flame that brought about the cooling smoke. It was trying to speak to her, and she knew that if she listened, the world would quiet down, the walls wouldn't close in so tight. It felt *familiar.*

Knock.

A dark figure sitting in the backseat appeared in the rearview mirror. At first, Abigail didn't believe her eyes, but then a streetlight revealed the man's features. She slammed on the brakes, and the car skidded to a stop in the middle of the road. She thought only of escape, to jump out and run, but when she turned her head to look into the backseat, no one was there. Yet, in the mirror, he was there: the old man. She recognized him. He was different now, more sinister, yet as real and alive as he once was all those years ago.

"You're dead," she whispered, not taking her eyes away from him. She felt ridiculous. Who was she speaking to? A ghost?

The old man grinned, black saliva pooling from the corners of his mouth. His head moved to either side in a taunting gesture. He mouthed her nickname, and she could almost hear it as if he'd spoken it aloud: Abby.

When Abigail reached for the door handle, a pain filled her throat like she'd swallowed scalding liquid. She coughed violently, covering her mouth out of reflex. Small splotches flecked her shaking palm. Blood?

Flashing lights filled the interior as a police car pulled up. The old man had vanished. However, the pungent smell of tobacco lingered in the air.

•••••••••••••

The flashlight beam forced Abigail to avert her eyes as the officer approached the rolled-down window. She turned off the car and kept her hands on the wheel, trying miserably to hide her unease.

"Everything all right, ma'am?" the officer asked from behind the hovering light.

"Yes. I just had a nervous breakdown or something."

The officer shone the light throughout the car. Abigail finally made out the officer's appearance: a short woman with a stocky build, her hair pulled back tightly and hidden under a hat. Her name tag read "Moore."

"License and registration." Abigail obliged. "Where you headed tonight?"

"Work. Up by Fort Campbell."

"You a soldier?"

"No, ma'am. I work at the Walmart near Gate 7."

"Last name... Rivers? Ain't you supposed to be rich or something? Why you working at Walmart?"

"You must be mistaken for someone else."

"Must be." The officer turned off the flashlight and clicked it into place on her belt. She handed back Abigail's documentation. "A nervous breakdown, you said? What's got you bothered with Christmas around the corner?"

"It's..." Abigail hadn't spoken to anyone other than the psychologist about what happened. She wasn't about to spill her guts to some random cop. "It's nothing really. Just the day-to-day grind of everything, you know?" *I'm losing my mind*, she thought.

"Yeah. I get it. Look, I'm going to let you go tonight. Just make sure you pull over to the curb next time. Okay?"

Abigail held back tears. "Yes, ma'am."

"Merry Christmas."

Officer Moore returned to her vehicle and shut off the flashing lights. The police car didn't move. It sat there as if waiting for another indicator of unlawful activity.

Abigail wiped away the tears that had snuck out without permission, then started the engine. Overly cautious with the cop watching, she continued down Fort Campbell Blvd until she crossed the Kentucky state line.

•••••••••••••

Abigail pulled into the Walmart parking lot. With the holidays fast approaching, it was busy despite the late hour. All the last-minute gift shopping was too hectic, and Abigail wished that if she could disappear for any two weeks out of the year, it'd be during the holiday shopping season.

The hustle and bustle was a constant reminder that everyone had their own lives and responsibilities. The days, weeks, and months all stacked on top of one another like sand in an oversized hourglass, forming an insurmountable pile that never let up because time didn't cease; it never flipped to flow the other direction because it didn't care about suffocating anyone under its unyielding pressure.

After the last drag of a cigarette, Abigail flicked it out of the cracked window before checking her mascara in the sunshade mirror. It wasn't perfect, never was. No one would notice; even if they did, she didn't care.

Before getting out of the car, Abigail peeked over her shoulder at the empty backseat. She felt an otherworldly aura, like the ghost stories her mother used to tell her. She missed those stories—no, not the stories. She missed her mother's raspy yet soothing voice. Abigail had thought it made her mother sound powerful. Too bad that power hadn't protected her in the end.

Abigail broke free from the painful memories, locked the car, and walked inside.

•••••••••••••

Thomas Traylor clawed his way out of the darkness and into the real world. Well, *his* world, the one he'd originally been born into. He gasped, the frozen air burning his lungs. This was the worst part, the rebirthing of his body through the hellish womb. It wasn't his first return, but every time was different, or, at least, *felt* different.

He got to his feet and surveyed his surroundings. He was behind a trailer home in the woods. It was strikingly similar to the mirrored world he'd escaped, except he much preferred natural trees and the lack of evil entities seeking to rend his flesh from his body.

Thomas was glad to have grabbed his jacket, for the snowfall was heavier here than in Nashville. But not by much. He was likely in the same hemisphere. Heck, the same state, by the looks of it.

He rounded the side of the trailer to the front. A truck sat in the driveway; someone was home. The "call" usually brought him to where he supposedly needed to be, but he hadn't figured out if it was a location-based pull or the person who needed him. The shape in the darkness had mentioned retrieving an imbued object, but he wasn't sure he understood exactly.

A glint caught his attention under the porch light. Shards of glass. A struggle or an accident? He bent down and picked up a piece, recognizing the shape as part of an ashtray. Voices drifted out of the front door—announcers on a sports channel.

Walking up the stairs, he could make out the living room, which was dimly lit by the blue flashing of a TV in the corner. Someone reclined in the chair, likely asleep. Not wanting to frighten the man by creepily standing on the front porch and staring in, he decided to knock and announce his presence.

"Sir," Thomas said. No response. "This is the police. I was hoping you could answer some questions. Sir?"

The man didn't move. That was when the bright light of a pharmaceutical commercial revealed the wounds on the man's face. He wasn't sleeping; he was hurt.

Thomas drew his pistol and opened the door, announcing his actions to anyone else who might be in the house. He scanned the small living space. Moving closer, he could tell that the man wasn't breathing. The head trauma had been severe. He decided to clear the house of potential threats before tending to the man for his own safety. The house was empty.

Returning to the living room, he stared down at the victim. His head had been caved in with a blunt object while he'd remained in a reclined position. The man had either been sleeping, or the killer was in the house with him and approached from one of the bedrooms—quick and brutal.

Was Thomas in the right place, but too late? Was he supposed to save this man? Regardless, the killer was out there, and Thomas needed to stop them. Not only because it was the right thing to do, but because the other side wouldn't cease its beckoning until he did.

•••••••••••••••

At 2 a.m., shoppers continued to mill about the Walmart aisles. Abigail worked the last open checkout lane, the only one with a lit number to not confuse the zombie patrons. One guy perused the chips wearing a hoodie and sunglasses, likely the son of a military officer stationed at Fort Campbell. Either he planned to steal something, or he was high. She hoped it was the latter because she hated thieves. She had to work minimum wage to put food on the table every week, while others got away with taking things for free. Abigail wasn't about to get injured, or worse, trying to stop someone desperate enough to steal potato chips.

Carl, Abigail's manager, devised reasons to chat her up most nights. His motives were never in question, but she just wasn't interested. As bad as Ricky was, at least she could escape him when she wanted.

A distressed young woman searched the medicine section. She found what she needed: an orange vitamin box. Abigail sympathized with the woman; the fear of childcare her main concern with starting a family. She wasn't opposed to the idea of children; she'd debated with Ricky about it for years, but their work schedules made the prospect of a tiny human entering their world terrifying.

The young woman shuffled by, averted her eyes, and continued right out of the front doors, never looking back. Abigail shook her head, but figured stealing medicine was somehow better justified than chips.

"Hey," someone said. Abigail jumped and turned to find Ricky. "Some people, am I right?"

Abigail scoffed. "Rick, what are you doing here? You've been drinking. The cops are out in force lately. You've got to be careful."

"Yeah, well, I was thinking about you. I feel terrible about how I've been acting the last few weeks. I know you need your space sometimes. I just... I'm not great at this kind of stuff, ya know?"

Abigail couldn't help but smile. Ricky wasn't a reflective person, so this was coming out of nowhere. She didn't know how to feel about it. Thankful?

"I... I'm sorry if I've been distant," she said, looking down. "I've been in my head too much, like I'm trying to escape the stupid world, but instead I surround myself with my stupid thoughts, and lately I can't figure out which is more stupid."

Her eyes met his, and she noticed something was off, like they were too glassy. No, that wasn't right. Foggy, maybe? They didn't seem to carry any life in them.

Ricky burped, then said, “Sounds about right. Could I get a pack of the Cane Blues while I’m here?”

Abigail flinched. She hadn’t expected that response, but this was Ricky. What *had* she expected? “Sure, one sec, Rick.”

She got a whiff of a strange smell emanating from him. It wasn’t the smell of alcohol. It bordered on putrid. She tried to ignore it as she opened the glass case behind her.

“Uh, I’ve only got Cane Platinums.”

“That’ll work.”

Abigail grabbed the small box and rang it up on the scanner. She looked up and froze. If before it had been his eyes, now it was his face, his cheeks sagging lower, the eyebrows a bit bushier.

“You all right, babe?” he asked, his voice a raspy whisper compared to what it had been.

“Rick,” she said, her voice shaky.

“Yes?”

“Is this real?”

“Of course, babe. Oh, you remember that noise you were worried about. I figured out what it was. Look.”

He lifted a hooked cane with an ornate handle and placed it on the counter. It pulled at her attention and held it there like a black hole might drag in the surrounding light, or, at least, that's how that eccentric astrophysicist explained it on that one science show she watched. The cane's handle was wet with a red liquid, and a clump of hair stuck to a curved section. She felt sick. A burning sensation lit up her chest, and she coughed uncontrollably.

Unconcerned with her condition, Ricky said, "Take a breath, sing a song. Eat a soul, move along. The world's nothin' but a burnin' bin, and she turns, turns, turns again. She floats along 'til she chokes, chokes, chokes. Seize 'em by their filtered throats, take a drag 'til there's nothin' left, grind 'em down into little motes, and leave her gasping for that final breath."

Abigail collapsed to the floor, her hands clutching at her neck. Boiling heat rose within her esophagus. When she coughed this time, black sludge peppered the white tile in clumps; the last thing she saw before blacking out.

•• · • · • • • · • · • •

"Can I see your ID, sir?" Officer Garrett asked, his breath cascading down the front of his uniform in the early morning frost. He held a notepad and a pen in his hands.

Sitting on the steps of the trailer home, Thomas produced a wallet and flipped it open, saying, "Detective Thomas Traylor, Nashville PD, Homicide."

Officer Garrett's eyes widened at that. Thomas put his badge away as two crime scene investigators squeezed by on the stairs and entered the front door.

The snow in the yard glistened with undisturbed crispness. Several police cars and a van were parked along the road and in the driveway. Thomas had been the one to call it in, even knowing how strange his presence appeared.

"How did you get here, Detective? I don't see your vehicle."

"I rode the bus."

"From Nashville?"

Thomas gritted his teeth, staring at the young officer. "Yes."

"What's your relationship to the victim?"

"No relation."

"No relation to the victim," the officer said, writing it down. "Forgive me, Detective, but did you have a reason to be here? Are you in Clarksville for an investigation? If so, why come to the Rivers' home?"

Rivers. The name was well-known. Was it a coincidence? Another police cruiser pulled into the driveway, and a familiar face stepped out.

"Sir?" the young officer asked to regain his attention.

"I was just passing through."

"What—"

"Officer Garrett, thank you for your thoroughness. I'll take it from here." Sergeant Benjamin Williams stood beside him and smiled. "Tom and I go way back."

Garrett looked from his superior to the detective, then put away his notepad and reluctantly walked away.

Sergeant Williams said, "How 'bout we go for a ride, Tom?"

•••••••••••••

The two men sat quietly while Williams drove. The curved country roads calmed Thomas, a nice reprieve from driving in the big city.

Clarksville had grown since Thomas's last visit, the nearby military base likely bringing in new families and new money.

"You hungry?" Williams asked.

"I could eat."

"Perfect. I know a spot."

They pulled up to a small gas station that looked abandoned except for the pillar of smoke emanating from the back. The gas pumps weren't operational, but several pickup trucks were in the small lot.

"Best BBQ in town and most people don't even know it exists," Williams said. "Hope you don't mind it this early."

"I never turn down an opportunity to eat," Thomas said.

They got their brisket sandwiches and returned to the police cruiser. Thomas wasn't sure why, but traveling through the other side made him ravenous. He thought of the creatures shaped like men running through the spiked woods... coming to devour him.

"How are you doing these days, Tom?" Williams asked.

"I'm fine."

"I mean, you seem fine, but that's not what I'm asking. How are you doing, *really*?"

Thomas didn't know how to answer that. He hadn't spoken to anyone about his wife leaving or about the... accident. He'd dove into the work to keep his mind off the heartache, even after the transfer out of the department. That's when the knocking had arrived, that's when he realized there was another world more evil than our own. Barely.

"I'm... not sure, Ben." Thomas stared out at the dense trees lining the country road. "I feel like I'm going crazy. Like the more time passes, the less I believe in what's true. That this is all some bad dream, and I can't wake up because life is the dream. I'm afraid the only thing worth living for is gone for good, and I'm just trying to hold onto a ghost."

Williams focused on the road as a disturbing report came in about one of their own. The details were sparse over the radio. He redirected his route to meet the officers at the scene. Thomas, of course, didn't mind the temporary distraction.

"I'm sorry for how it all went down, Tom. I truly am. There's nothing I can say that can bring her back, but I want you to know that I'm here for you if you ever need to talk. You have my number. And for what it's worth, I believed you."

Thomas nodded. "Thanks, Ben. I appreciate it."

They eventually pulled into a quiet neighborhood where police cruisers had their flashers going. A firetruck and an ambulance were also on the scene.

"Oh, no," Williams said. "Please, no."

Thomas remained silent. He'd lost fellow officers, his friends, before. He knew the emptiness that followed all too well.

They got out of the car and walked up to the house, where a deputy stopped them.

"Is Moore okay?" Williams asked.

"No, sir," the deputy said, unsure of how to phrase it. "She was... killed last night in her sleep, along with her family."

"Killed? How? The hell is going on?"

"We don't have all the details yet. Initial conclusion was murder-suicide. It's pretty grim in there. Too early to say, sir."

Williams cursed, then looked at Thomas with rage in his eyes.

"All right, Tom. You just happen to show up, and my city starts to fall apart. Tell me why you're really back."

•••••••••••••

When Abigail awoke, a nearby voice called to someone. She looked over but couldn't see who had spoken because sunlight sliced through the blinds. The silhouette stepped forward to block the harsh light, allowing Abigail's eyesight to adjust. It was Carl, fake-smiling down at her. His hair was disheveled, and his eyes were baggy, framed with dark half moons.

"Hey, Abby, how are you feeling?" She struggled to speak. "Take it easy. From what I hear, you need a lot of rest."

A nurse entered the room and checked Abigail's vitals. "I'll get Doctor Ramirez in here for you in a sec, honey."

The nurse left. Abigail pointed to her throat to see if Carl knew anything.

He shook his head. "I'd rather let the doctor explain it."

She had always thought Carl was a creep, but the fact that he was there and Ricky wasn't screamed volumes. Where was he, anyway? Surely the hospital would have attempted to contact him. She had a vague memory of him being at the store. Had that been a dream?

The doctor entered the room. “Abigail Rivers. Good to see you awake. I’m Dr. Ramirez,” he said. “Do you mind if I call you Abigail?”

She shook her head. She preferred it, actually.

“Great. How are you feeling? Do you need anything?”

“No, I’m okay,” she said with a rasp.

“That’s good to hear. Well, I’m sure you’re wondering why you’re in the hospital on Fort Campbell. I do have some bad news, Abigail. I’m not going to sugarcoat it. We believe you have adenocarcinoma of the lungs. It’s a type of cancer that affects moisture glands in the body and spreads when the glands grow out of control. I say ‘believe’ because we’ll need to run some more tests to be sure. We’re testing a sample of your blood as we speak, and have scheduled you for X-rays. Abigail, are you a smoker?”

Abigail nodded again, her eyes watering up.

“I thought so. Most of my patients are. I want you to know that we’ve caught it early enough for it to be treatable. It’s going to be a tough fight, but you look like a fighter.” He smiled momentarily. “Though I advise you to quit smoking immediately. This should be a wake-up call for you, but some of my patients choose to live their own way, and I can't force them to change their habits. It's up to you to fight the addiction just as your body fights off the cancer. Does that make sense?"

Abigail stared blankly past the doctor's shoulder at the large picture frame hanging on the wall behind him. It was a landscape portrait of the Great Smoky Mountains, but the glass reflected the room in an almost mirror-image, and she stared at the back of the doctor's head as if she was watching this all play out like a movie or an out-of-body experience.

"I've seen this before, Abigail. You will overcome it. But half the battle will be from the inside," Dr. Ramirez said, tapping his index finger at the center of his chest.

She didn't respond. Carl stood awkwardly by, unsure of how to act naturally in the situation. The doctor regarded him for the first time.

"If you don't mind me asking, what is your relation to Abigail?"

Before Carl could respond, Abigail said, "He's my boss."

"Shift Manager," Carl corrected.

Dr. Ramirez smiled. "Ah, the Walmart outside the gate, right? I thought I recognized you. Well, it's nice of you to show your support for Abigail. She will need every bit of it." The doctor turned back to her. "Do you have any family or relatives I can call?"

"My boyfriend—" a knock at the door. The nurse returned.

"Doctor, there's an officer here who wants to speak with the patient."

Abigail recognized Officer Moore standing in the hallway.

"Just a second, Stacy. I'll be right out," Dr. Ramirez said. "Abigail, remember, you're a fighter. You'll get through this."

The doctor flashed his brilliant, white-toothed smile before heading for the door. He stepped outside the room and spoke briefly with the officer before heading down the hallway. Officer Moore entered and closed the door. She walked up to the side of the bed before asking Carl to leave. Carl looked at Abigail, who nodded reassuringly. He left them alone.

"You've had quite the rough night," Moore said.

"I've had worse." Abigail meant it.

Moore looked down at the floor before saying, "I figured since we met not too long ago, I'd be the one to tell you."

Abigail furrowed her brow. "Tell me what?"

"It's your boyfriend, Ricky. He's... he's gone."

Abigail tried to interpret every meaning of 'gone' other than the one she knew to be true. "Is he—"

"He's dead, Abby. He was murdered in your home."

Abigail sat up. Her gaze darted to the picture frame on the wall behind the officer. The reflection in the glass was... *off*. It no longer depicted the starkness of a hospital, but a charred husk of the building. Worse, the reflection of the person talking to her wasn't Officer Moore.

"It was easy bashing his head in. He never even saw it coming—"

Abigail's heart rate skyrocketed. The bedside monitor beeped and flashed. The room darkened as the cop leaned in, a crooked smile on the crooked face pretending to be Officer Moore.

"—and you won't either, not when I'm ready to take you, to take your breath. To make you mine, like you've always been. To make you shine like a cigarette end."

Her vision failed her, and her head fell back against the pillow. She struggled to remain conscious as the nurse rushed in to check on her. Officer Moore's normal voice returned, explaining that poor Abigail couldn't handle the sad news of Ricky's passing. The rapid beeping of the machine filled her mind, and it morphed into knocking, the knocking of a cane down the inescapable corridor of her impending death.

••·•·••••·•·••

Abigail coughed herself awake. The hospital room was empty, and the sunlight that had once snuck through the blinds was all but gone. She sobbed in the semi-darkness, remembering Ricky. How could she trust the source of the information? She couldn't, but Abigail knew in her heart that it was true.

An ache erupted within her, not one of pain but of longing—a yearning for a small, lightweight stick filled with nicotine, the fixation of it pressed up against her lips, the smoke filling her with its calm serenity.

There was a knock on the door. Wide-eyed, Abigail waited for someone to open it. No one entered.

"Carl?" she asked, her voice cracking.

A second knock, more like a hammer strike, then a third. The door shook in its frame with each impact. A fourth thud made the wall groan as if from a massive presence. The handle twisted, and the door creaked inward until it bumped against the far wall. There was no one on the other side, except the cane hanging from the outer knob, which faced her in the hospital bed. Faint laughter echoed from the hallway, and the fluorescent lights quivered, barely alive. Then, a gravelly voice entered her mind:

A world awaits, full of fateful mistakes, and the one who wishes fails to take the cake.

Abigail removed the monitors clinging to her skin and got out of bed. Standing was difficult, and the floor was ice cold on her bare feet. The temperature in the building had dropped suddenly, her breath pluming in front of her. Frost crept across the small window in the door.

Who will you be at the bitter end, where the snakes wait right 'round the bend?

Abigail called out for a nurse. None answered. She walked to the doorway, her feet briefly sticking to the frozen floor. The cane dangled there on the door handle, taunting her.

Become what they fear and shake loose the tears; break free of the rust that clogs the gears.

Abigail grabbed the cane. It was heavier than it looked. She turned it horizontally. Two equidistant slits had been carved into it, positioned over a larger, crooked line snaking its way underneath. They opened; two eyes and a sickly mouth.

Abigail flinched, wanting to drop the cane but unable. It was as if her hands had melded with it. The face laughed, black tar drooling out of the parted lips. It spat in her face, forcing her to close her eyes, and she had to use her forearm to wipe away the filth. When she reopened them, *he* stood before her, the harsh, flickering light from the hallway casting menacing shadows that darkened his features. A thick line of sickly goo trailed the tile between his feet.

"Take a breath, sing a song."

He stepped closer.

"What do you want from me?"

"Eat a soul, move along."

Abigail backed into the bed and could go no farther.

"The world's nothin' but a burnin' bin, and she turns, turns, turns again."

The old man spat with each word—the rising static in Abigail's ears on the verge of deafening.

Abigail raised the cane like a baseball bat, the face in the shaft grinning.

"I'll do it again, I swear."

"She floats along 'til she chokes, chokes, chokes!"

He lunged at her on the final word. She swung and struck him on the temple. He fell to the floor in a heap. The static died away in a flash, and so did the icy layer covering the room. She stood over the body of Carl, lying motionless on the floor, blood pooling beneath his head.

Abigail tried to scream, but a knot in her throat prevented any noise from escaping.

•••••••••••••

They found Abigail kneeling over Carl's body; the bloody cane tossed on the bed. A nurse called base security forces, who apprehended her with no resistance and moved her to a vacant room on the same floor, handcuffing her to the bed.

She stared at the clock on the far wall, which displayed 2:33 a.m. The door opened. The soldier standing guard let in another man and closed the door.

"Miss Rivers," the man said. She didn't respond. "Glad to see that you're still awake. I'm Detective Thomas Traylor."

The clock's second hand ticked on, each notch sounding like a heavy thud in her mind.

"It sounds like your life has fallen apart in the last twenty-four hours. Either that, or it's been crumbling for some time, and we're just now seeing the debris."

Abigail looked up. The detective was middle-aged with a thick beard. His Tennessee drawl was comforting. He stepped closer.

Abigail picked at the hospital tag on her wrist. She breathed in a deep, jagged breath and exhaled slowly. "Do I need a lawyer?"

"Yes, Miss Rivers, you will need to get a lawyer. Eventually. But you and I both know a lawyer isn't going to save you from what's haunting you. I've seen it, too. The darkness that forces you to do things you don't want to do."

Abigail shook her head. He was coercing her into saying something incriminating. She'd seen it on a show once, and she wouldn't fall into that trap.

"I didn't do what you think I did. Whatever that happens to be."

"Okay, look, I get it. You don't trust me, but I'm here for you, not the investigation. I mean, they're two sides to the same coin, but hopefully I can help you and we can figure this thing out together." Detective Traylor spied a chair in the corner of the room. He dragged it over and sat. "Man, I wish I had a smoke. Just the end of a Cane's, like a puff and a half."

Abigail closed her eyes. A headache, tapping faintly on the inside of her skull, came into focus at the mention of Cane's. When was the last time she had a smoke?

"Speaking of Cane's," he continued, "that name's famous around here. Mr. Lionel Cane was a prominent figure, and his passing equally notable." Abigail remained silent, one hand squeezing the other to prevent them from shaking. "His maid, right? Bludgeoned him with his own cane until his face was unrecognizable. Mr. Cane killed by a cane. How ironic."

The detective stood and put the chair back. He lingered at the picture frame, watching her through the reflection. She checked to see if he was looking at her. He spoke again when she looked away.

"Something, or someone, depending on what you believe, called me here to help you, Miss Rivers."

Abigail furrowed her brow as she rubbed her elbow, not knowing how to react. "I don't understand what you mean."

He turned to her. "I believe you do. You've seen something, haven't you, Miss Rivers? It's plaguing you, and you aren't sure why. You feel like you can't tell anyone because you'll be locked up forever with no hope of escape. They'll think you're crazy. Making it all up so you can get a lighter sentence. But the crazy part is that you're the only sane one willing to accept the truth, that there are darker forces out there working against us at every turn."

A tear fell down her cheek unbidden. "Y-yes. But how do you—"

"Because I've lived it. Still am, actually. And I might be the only person who can help you. So, Miss Rivers, are you going to tell me who or what is terrorizing you?"

Abigail couldn't explain it, but she felt at home in his presence, like she could tell him anything, and that no matter how insane it sounded, he would support her. She'd never felt that way before. Not even with her mom.

Before she could talk herself out of it, she said, "The man you were talking about. It's him, Mr. Cane, but older than I remember. He was nice at first, back when he was alive, I mean. He would read me bedtime stories and make up rhymes that made me laugh. But then we started staying at his big house some nights. We'd play games of Hide and Seek, but when I stopped wanting to play, he would force me into the closet and forget about me. I could still hear them sometimes, and when I cried, he would frighten and beat me. My mother tried to stop him, but he threatened to kill us both. He would use his cane to..."

"I'm so sorry to hear that, Miss Rivers. I didn't know you were involved."

"It's fine, Detective. No one does. Most people are only aware of the settlement. Money is all anyone cares about. Funny thing is, I got none of it. The lawyers did. I was just a child. And now, even though he's dead, Mr. Cane has been following me, taking the form of other people sometimes."

"Other people?"

Abigail nodded. "He appeared to me as the officer who stopped me when I was driving to work—"

"Moore?"

"Yes. And earlier, he attacked me in the hospital room... it wasn't Carl. It was *him*. He kept coming at me. I told him to stop. He wouldn't. It all happened so fast."

"And you're sure it's him? Mr. Cane, I mean."

"I'm certain."

"Even though your mother killed him?"

Abigail didn't respond. Detective Traylor stroked his beard as he crossed the room to pull back the curtain and peer outside. He looked like a felon searching for a suspicious van. He let the curtain fall back.

"Who else spoke to the imposter Moore, the one who came to you here in the hospital?"

"The nurse and the doctor, maybe."

"Your doctor? Are you sure?"

"Yes, I'm pretty sure."

"Okay, Miss Rivers, I have to go somewhere for a little while."

"Don't leave me. Not now. Please."

"I'm not leaving you. I'll be right back."

She'd finally let someone in, and he was going to leave her. Who else did she have? They were all gone.

"What if he comes back? What if he kills me?"

"I won't let that happen. I promise."

The detective opened the door in a hurry. He spoke to the soldier outside, then gave Abigail one last reassuring nod before leaving her alone in the cold, dark room.

•• · • · •• • •• · • ·••

Thomas jogged to the reception desk, where a lone nurse sat at a computer.

"Abigail Rivers' doctor, have they been notified of the situation?"

"Uh, yes. We called Dr. Ramirez and informed him. He said he'd be in first thing in the morning to check on her. He usually gets in early. Is everything okay, sir?"

"No. Call him again." When she looked at him skeptically, he added, "Please."

"You're going to have to give me more than that for me to call him again, sir. Is this an emergency?"

"Yes," he yelled, slamming his palm down on the counter. He instantly regretted it. Her eyes were wide, but she clearly had dealt with unruly patients and family members before.

"One moment, sir." The nurse picked up the phone and dialed a number, keeping the detective in her peripheral vision. It rang for a long time. She hung up. "He's not available at this time. What's the emergency? Or will I need to call the cops—"

"I am a cop. Where does he live? He might be in danger. I need to get to him now."

"Danger? What do you mean? And you don't look like a cop."

Thomas produced his badge and asked again, as calmly as he could manage.

●•·●·•·●•·•●·•●

Thomas charged down the hospital steps to Williams' parked car. He opened the door and hopped in, panting. "It's the doctor. We've got to get to the doctor."

"The hell you talking about?" Officer Williams asked.

"If we don't get to the girl's doctor soon, this Dr. Ramirez, he's going to be murdered by a shape-shifting demon, which will then kill everyone it comes in contact with until it takes

Abigail's soul once and for all. You need more info? Let's go." Thomas buckled his seatbelt.

Williams stared for a moment before saying, "Dang it, Tom. You didn't mention shape-shifting demons when I asked you why you came to Clarksville. If you had, I wouldn't have been so eager to help."

"Exactly, which is why I didn't bring it up. But now we don't have time to debate it. Let's go, Ben."

Sergeant Williams started the engine. "Sure. Fine, whatever. Glorified taxi driver now. Where's this damn demon doctor's house?"

••·•·••·•·••·•·••

Knock.

Abigail sat up in bed to see someone leaving her room. Looking around, she remembered where she was. The sterile hospital was marred by skulking shadows, the only reprieve coming from the pale finger of light curling in through the cracked door.

Knock.

The soldier no longer stood outside, but she could hear a muffled voice out in the hallway, and she thought she recognized it.

Knock.

When had the detective left? Hours ago? He said he wouldn't leave her. It had all been a ruse to get a confession. Why had she believed him?

Knock.

The soft voice escalated into a surprised yell, and then something thudded in the hallway, followed by a chilling silence. Abigail wanted nothing more than to wake up from this nightmare.

Abigail lifted her hand, and the handcuff fell to clatter on the floor. Someone had wanted her free. She feared who that someone might be.

She got out of bed and stepped into the hallway, the lights flickering unnaturally. There was a mound on the floor in the center of the hall. It was the soldier. Another figure loomed over him with a surgical blade in hand, glinting in the phosphorescent lighting. Dr. Ramirez grinned, his face smeared with dark red, those white teeth gleaming between parted lips.

The overhead lights behind the doctor began exploding in rapid succession, drenching the hallway in a flood of darkness. Abigail spun and ran as the bulbs continued shattering in her direction down the rest of the corridor. The backup emergency lights came on, filtering the sharp corners and vacant doorways in their hellish hue. The sound of feet scuffing the tile neared behind her as she sprinted toward the elevator doors, their silvery sheen reflecting two red emergency lights like devil eyes watching her approach. She collided with the door and slammed a hand on the call button, searching behind her for signs of the doctor. He was nowhere to be seen, but his laugh filled the hallway, echoing. She considered dashing to the stairs, but the shadows seemed to swirl and beckon her forth.

The elevator opened, and she fell inside. With quivering hands, she pressed all the buttons just to get the doors to shut faster, which didn't seem to work. She didn't care what floor it took her as long as it was far away from there.

After the doors closed, the elevator jolted into motion, and both directional arrows lit up. Her inputs hadn't mattered, for it moved of its own volition, with her stuck inside. Trapped.

The silvery walls closed in, and so did her terror. The droning of the elevator morphed into that of air passing through a tunnel, a passage contracting and expanding, like breath through an esophagus. A light revealed itself before her, and she crawled to reach it, her reflection in the metal melting away to reveal a gateway. It was her salvation. It was... a bedroom.

Abigail recognized the room. She'd returned to the closet, the one he'd repeatedly forced her into all those years ago, the space full of boxes, clothes, and forgotten shoes tightening around her. She made to turn back, but her body failed to respond to her mind. She felt powerless, just as she had as a young girl.

Through the crack in the closet doors, the old man, not so old then, forced her mother onto the bed. Abigail watched as the cane dropped to the floor; he'd needed one ever since the war, or so her mother had said. Abigail tried to stifle her sobs with fingers so tight against her lips that it hurt. Then, he stood from the bed and limped over.

"Abby, Abby, Abby," he said, crouching. "If you don't quiet down, you'll stay in the closet all night like last time, ya hear?"

Hearing his voice again broke her completely, and she sobbed even louder. He yanked open the door, grabbed her by the hair, and dragged her out. She slid across the carpet, her arms and legs burning. Her fingers brushed something, and she grabbed onto it like a lifeline, which indeed it was.

She swung it wildly, connecting with a soft thud. *One.* He grunted and stumbled. Abigail got to her feet. Mr. Cane was now eye level with her on one knee. She swung his cane at his snarling face. *Two.* He fell; she hit him again. *Three.* Her mother screamed, but Abigail didn't hear it. Each swing had beaten away her fear. He looked up at her with one swelling eye and a devilish grin. It had been the only way not to feel the overwhelming dread that had overcome her—the only way to save them both. She brought it down one final time. *Four.*

The elevator gears ground to a halt. The bedroom had vanished, and despite herself, she didn't want the doors to open. But they did, like curtains revealing a theater's stage, an empty stage underneath a blackened ceiling. The only light emanated from inside the elevator, but as she peered out, she saw the chamber was vast, yet completely enclosed, like a cavern deep underground. If that hadn't worried her, the moving walls and ceiling made her sick to her stomach. The living cavern dripped black tar in lengthy columns like stalactites, and moaning, faceless figures reached out desperately from their gelatinous prison.

Abigail pressed herself against the back of the elevator, the metal cold as ice on her skin. She refused to leave, despite its suffocating closeness on all sides.

An oily blob splattered onto the platform just outside the elevator. It bubbled like heated chocolate, steam rising from the expanding pool. Something moved inside. No, not some*thing*, some*one*. An arm burst from the black sludge. A head emerged next, and as the tar slipped from the face, she questioned the impossibility of it all.

"Going somewhere, Abby," Mr. Cane said, laughing.

Abigail had become frozen with fear as he extricated himself from the black goo. A voice within told her to get up, to fight. So, she forced herself to move. She reached out and pressed the button, and the doors began to close, but Mr. Cane's foot stepped between them, and they reopened. He was larger than before, no longer an old man. Despite this, he leaned upon the cane to keep upright.

"I sold my soul once," he said to her. "I know I can't get mine back, but yours... yours is ripe for the taking, Abby. And I've been waiting a long time for this moment. All I had to do was wait."

Mr. Cane grabbed her by the ankle and dragged her from the elevator like the young girl being dragged from the closet. His strength had become inhuman. She screamed, not from the pain of her back scraping but because her nightmare was manifesting once more.

"Knock, knock, knock, knooock," he said, flipping her over.

He raised the cane and hit her with it. Memories flooded her mind with each strike, but Abigail wasn't a child any longer. She was a fighter, always had been.

She kicked him in the knee, the bad one that he favored. He yelled as he toppled over, the cane falling from his grasp. She twisted and scrambled for the elevator, but the doors had closed.

"Oh, Abby, always struggling, always running, never facing reality," he said, his voice shifting into a female's. "Face me for once!"

Abigail looked back, and her mother stood in Mr. Cane's place. She was smoking a cigarette in her nightgown, ragged and unkempt.

"You blame me, don't you? You blame me for your problems. You think the world is out to get you, that you have no say in what happens because you're bogged down by all the garbage everyone else is doing, that you can't breathe from the pressure of it all. Is that it? Poor Abby can't breathe. Poor, poor Abby."

Her mother never called her Abby. Her mother was dead. She knew that, but....

"Aw, just look at her. Poor Abby needs a smoke. And she needs Momma to give it to her." Her mother grabbed Abigail by the shirt and lifted her against the wall next to the elevator doors. Abigail couldn't break free; its strength was unmatched. Her mother forced the butt end of the cigarette up against her lips. "Go on, Abby, breathe it in. Trust me. It'll feel good. All of your worries will just fade away."

Abigail twisted her head back and forth to avoid the cigarette, but the hand presenting it followed her mouth wherever she moved. She pushed against the impostor, but she had no leverage.

"Smoke the damn cigarette," her mother yelled.

Tears ran down Abigail's cheeks as her willpower began to fail. Maybe it wouldn't be that bad. Maybe she would feel better. Maybe it would end the pain.

The elevator dinged. Her impostor mother's eyes went wide, looking at the opening doors. A man stepped out, pointing a pistol in her direction.

"Let her go," Detective Traylor said.

Abigail's impostor mother did just that and stepped back. Abigail slid to the ground, rubbing her neck where the elbow had pressed in hard. When she looked up, it was no longer her mother, but Dr. Ramirez with a bloody smile.

"I heard you were looking for me, Detective. Well, here I am. I'm doing just fine."

"I always hated dealing with doctors," Thomas said. He glanced over at Abigail. "You okay, Miss Rivers? Told you I wouldn't leave you." She nodded, still rubbing her neck. "Look, Demon Thing, I already found the real doctor. What was left of him anyway. So, no need for the charade."

The doctor's expression shifted from mocking to one of anger. Pure evil resided behind that human façade.

"How did you get here? This is *my* world," the doctor said.

"I have my ways of getting around," Thomas said.

"Ah, you must be one of them," the doctor said. "I figured someone like you would come around eventually. Not that it matters. You'll die like all the rest."

The doctor's skin sloughed off like a reptile shedding its dead layers, and a skeleton of black tar writhed in its place. The jaw drooped, and its eyes shone red. The chamber took on a bloodied hue during the transformation, the ooze quivering overhead.

"Dang. You're uglier than I imagined."

The demon crouched in preparation to jump. The detective unloaded the entire pistol magazine into the demon's center mass. The 9 millimeter bullets slammed into the skeletal frame but did nothing to slow it. The demon lunged and Thomas rolled to the side, barely escaping its clawed hand slashing at his head. He rose to one knee and released the pistol's magazine with a flick, replacing it with another in a fluid maneuver. He fired again, this time one clear shot at close range into the creature's gooey temple. Nothing. It turned its head slowly to look at him before backhanding him in the chest. He flew across the strange platform to skid to a stop near the edge.

Abigail stood. She would not be able to live with herself if the detective died protecting her. The demon had been right about one thing: she had been looking for a way to numb the pain. But everything hurting her was right here, and it was her turn to fight back.

The demon grabbed the detective by the foot to dangle him upside down like defenseless prey. It moved to the edge to send him over the side. Before it could dispense of him, it buckled over with a guttural moan. It faced Abigail, who held the cane above her knee. A splintered crack had formed across the face embedded in the cane. The demon dropped the detective back onto the platform, a forgotten plaything, and stepped closer to her, arms raised.

The carved mouth spoke, "You cannot defeat me, Abby. I'll always be there, knocking, waiting for you to answer." The demon prepared to lunge for her.

"Oh yeah? Knock on this, Old Man."

Abigail slammed the cane down on her knee. It split in half with a crack that shook the pulsing chamber. The now-separated eyes rolled back into the two halves of the cane before disappearing. She grinned.

Surprisingly, the demon seemed unaffected this time. Hot breath steamed out of its blackened teeth as it stared at her. Those red eyes blazed brighter, molten and full of Hell's hatred.

Abigail's grin faded. "Oh no."

"Over here, Miss Rivers," the detective yelled. Abigail glanced in the direction of his voice. He'd reached the elevator.

The demon leapt. She dove out of the way as it crashed into the rocky platform where she'd stood. Her side ached, but still holding onto the two halves of the cane, she scrambled to her feet to run to the open elevator. The detective fired the rest of his magazine into the thing chasing her with little effect as the thudding footsteps continued to gain on her. He hit the button to close the doors as she fell inside. It wasn't fast enough to keep the demon out. It clambered inside the small space, and the doors shut, trapping them all together.

The demon knocked the detective to the side and grabbed Abigail's arm to pull her close. Its touch burned her bare skin with a sizzle, and she screamed. Its dripping mouth opened wide to consume her face. Immobilized, she closed her eyes, accepting a fate that never came.

Abigail opened them again to find the demon had returned to its human form, that of Mr. Cane. The detective held him in a headlock, pulling him back away from her.

"How are you doing this?" Mr. Cane asked.

"You're in *my* world now," Detective Traylor said.

The detective twisted Mr. Cane off of Abigail and pressed him against the reflective wall of the elevator. Mr. Cane's eyes glowed brighter at the sight of himself, murderous and scathing. Thomas didn't see the surgical blade materialize in the old man's right hand. It jabbed up and struck him in the shoulder. The detective grunted as the old man yanked the blade out in a spray of blood. The detective staggered down to one knee, staunching the bleeding with one hand, while maintaining contact with his other.

Mr. Cane turned with a sinister look, blade raised, his murderous gaze on Abigail. Then, his eyes went wide as she slammed the splintered halves of the cane into his chest and neck. He fell back against the wall, and his features morphed into an amalgamation of everyone he'd killed: Ricky, Carl, Moore, and Ramirez. He shuddered and convulsed, something wicked happening internally; a seething, sucking, grotesque bubbling that contorted his entire frame into an inhuman bloat.

"Knock, knock, knock..." Mr. Cane stopped, his eyes bulging. A faint rasp of air seeped past his blistering lips as he said it one final time, "Knooooock."

The old man exploded, his body popping like a water balloon. Except, instead of red blood, his insides contained the same black liquid that had coated the otherworldly chamber they had escaped. It splattered across Abigail and the detective with a hot splash, painting the elevator walls in an obsidian paste.

Abigail, covered in sticky filth, found that she could no longer breathe. She grabbed at her throat in futility. The blockage could not be reached because it was inside her, in her lungs.

"You okay, Miss Rivers?" Detective Traylor asked, standing and nearly slipping in the muck. "Miss—"

She couldn't hear him. The walls closed in. The closet, the darkness. It was suffocating. There was no escape, there would never be an escape.

"Just breathe, Abigail. Take a breath."

Abigail fell to her hands and knees. She recalled what Mr. Cane had said to her: "I sold my soul once. I know I can't get mine back, but yours is ripe for the taking, Abby." He had infected her like he said he would. He was *inside* her, always had been. This was the end.

"The Lord is my shepherd; I shall not want," the detective said, resting one hand on her back. "He lays me down in green pastures: he leads me beside still waters. He restores my soul: leads me in the paths of righteousness for his name's sake."

Abigail choked, coughed. It hurt, but at least air had gotten through. She focused on the detective's words as he spoke.

"Yea, though I walk through the valley of the shadow of death, I will fear no evil: for thou art with me; thy rod and thy staff comfort me. Thou preparest a table before me in the presence of my enemies: thou anointest my head with oil; my cup runneth over."

It burned like liquid fire, but she heaved, and black tar poured from her mouth like vomit. She welcomed the terrible pain with tears of joy.

"Surely goodness and mercy shall follow me all the days of my life: and I will dwell in the house of the Lord forever."

By the end of his prayer, there was nothing left to expel, and she finally sucked in a ragged, fiery breath. Dizziness overcame her then, and the world blurred.

The last thing she saw was the detective lowering her to the wet ground, his lips moving inaudibly, the doors to the elevator opening, others with flashlights peering in and hovering above her, their glow like that of angels. Then their lights vanished, and darkness stamped out the pain.

•••••••••••••••

A light rain fell over the cemetery. The weather had warmed enough to exist in that in between of rain or snow. A gathering, dressed in all black, sat under a pop-up tent, watching as the machine lowered the casket into the ground. Soft sobs rose over the patter of raindrops hitting the tent's fabric. A man walked over from the nearby street and sat down in an empty chair next to a dry-eyed woman.

"How are you holding up, Miss Rivers?"

Abigail briefly smiled. "Still breathing, Detective."

"I'm glad to hear it."

"How's your shoulder?"

"Healing. Thanks."

They sat in silence before Abigail asked, "How did you know it would work?"

"What?"

"The words you spoke that saved my life."

Thomas thought for a minute. "It was probably less the words and more that you'd made your decision."

"Decision?"

Dirt spilled into the hole to cover the casket. The sobbing increased, Ricky's mother collapsing into her husband's embrace. Thunder rumbled overhead. The detective removed something from underneath his collar and lifted it over his head. He studied the cross resting in his palm for a moment before handing it to her. She took it reluctantly.

"To fight," he said.

Abigail gave him an understanding smile as he stood. She grabbed the sleeve of his jacket. He leaned over so she could speak into his ear.

"Thank you for coming back."

He nodded to her before jogging through the heavy rain to Sergeant William's police cruiser.

"She doing all right?" Williams asked as Thomas sat in the passenger seat and shut the door.

"Define 'all right?' Poor thing has a long road ahead of her. But she's doing better than when I found her. That's a win in my book."

"Good way of looking at it. So, what now? Got any more demons you want to tell me about?"

Detective Traylor had plenty of demons, but now wasn't the time to disclose the details.

"I'd like to go home."

Williams scoffed. "Glorified taxi."

•••••••••••••

Several weeks passed before the next call from the other side. Thomas Traylor entered the standing mirror to find himself surrounded by jagged mountain ranges on all sides. He walked down a hill to the edge of a river of black sludge flowing alongside a walking path that led under a bridge—a shape writhed in the shadows, its familiar voice emanating from the tunnel.

"Hello again, Mister," the shape said. "Did you get what I asked for?"

Detective Traylor presented the two halves of the broken cane. The shape's glass-like grin returned, its eyes glistening with excitement.

"You'll have to come out to get it," Thomas said.

The shape hesitated, its inky smile disappearing.

"Come on," Thomas said. "I trusted you enough to crawl under a trailer home. You can trust me enough to take this relic, which I worked so hard to find, for you. We're friends, right?"

"Friends?" the shape said, unsure. "You are a friend? Yes."

The shape crawled out of the shadow of the bridge on all fours to approach the detective. Underneath all of the hair and rags was someone he thought he'd never see again.

The shape tilted its matted head, then held out its hands. The detective dropped to his knees and embraced it. The shape fought him for a moment before acquiescing. A young girl materialized from the shadows that had masked her appearance. Thomas' touch, his strange ability, had brought her back.

"Friend?" his daughter asked.

"Yes, Claire," Thomas said. "And I'm here to bring you home."

MEET THE AUTHORS

Rose Biggin is a writer and performer based in London. Her first short fiction collection is forthcoming from NewCon Press and her novels are punk fantasy Wild Time (Surface Press) and gothic thriller The Belladonna Invitation (Ghost Orchid).

•••••••••••••

Hamish Kavanagh is a New Zealand writer, currently based in the UK. He has recently completed his first full length novel a dystopian mystery. This is currently out for submission with literary agents. Hamish typically writes speculative fiction, erring towards darker subjects. His stories often take a thought experiment shape which leaves readers pondering the ideas raised long after reading. His shorter work has featured in the Vexed to Nightmare anthology and has recently had a story accepted for publication in the Well's Street Journal literary journal.

●•·•·•·•●•·•·•●·•·•●

Clark Boyd lives and works in The Netherlands. His previous work has appeared in various horror, science fiction, and mystery anthologies. Before trying his hand at fiction, Clark spent more than 20 years covering international news for public radio in the U.S.

•••••••••••••

Leigh Parrish's true identity is a closely-guarded secret. Whether this is because her true form is so horrifying that your mind can't comprehend it, or just because she prefers not having her real name tied to her fiction is a matter of debate to this day.

•••••••••••••

Rachel Henderson lives in New Orleans, where she spends her free time writing and playing bagpipes. Her stories have appeared or are forthcoming in Neither Fish Nor Foul, Epic Echoes, NYC Midnight, the Creepy podcast, Finn McCool's Short Story Anthology and The Writer's Arena. In 2021, she won first place in the NYC Midnight Short Screenplay Competition. Find her at www.rlhendie.com.

•••••••••••••

Warren Benedetto writes dark fiction about horrible people, horrible places, and horrible things. He is an award-winning author who has published over 275 stories, appearing in publications such as Dark Matter Magazine, Fantasy Magazine, and The Dread Machine; on podcasts such as The NoSleep Podcast, Tales to

Terrify, and Chilling Tales For Dark Nights; and in anthologies from Apex Magazine, Tenebrous Press, Scare Street, and many more. He also works in the video game industry, where he holds 55+ patents for various types of gaming technology. For more information, visit warrenbenedetto.com and follow @warrenbenedetto on Twitter and Instagram.

Sam Crain lives in Fremont, California. Now that she's finished her PhD in English, she's free to return to her first love, writing stories, which she does whenever she can steal her pens back from her cats. Her most recent publication is "Frank the Dragon," forthcoming from Sheila-na-Gig.

•••••••••••••

Matthew Christian is a writer hailing from the farmlands of Wisconsin. His work has been published in various online outlets and he actively publishes independent fiction to his Substack (https://targetednightmares.substack.com/).

•••••••••••••

Born in Ukraine and currently residing in California, Elana Gomel is an academic, an award-winning writer, and a professional nomad. She is well-known in the academy for her work on speculative fiction and narrative theory, including books such as Science Fiction,

Alien Encounters, and the Ethics of Posthumanism: Beyond the Golden Rule and The Palgrave Handbook of Global Fantasy. Twelve years ago, she published her first fantasy novel and has never looked back since. She is the author of a hundred and fifty published short stories, two collections, several novellas, and eight novels. Her stories appeared in Best Horror of the Year, The Dark magazine, Apex and many anthologies. Her latest novels are Nightwood, a fairy tale about marriage and monsters (Silver Award in the Bookfest 2023 contest) and Nine Levels, a mythological fantasy.

Pip Pinkerton was born and raised in Oakdale, Minnesota. Pip is a wanderer and a dreamer. He loves writing short stories, poetry, and screenplays. A former theatre student and current guitar player, Pip currently co-manages a record shop. When he is not writing or jamming, he is spending time with his trusty rottweiler Shrimp. Pip has been published on the Monstrous Femme website, as well as on HorrorAdd icts.net, and with Wicked Shadow Press. He has upcoming stories to be featured in anthologies by Dark Moon Rising Publications, J. Manfred Weichsel publishing, and Ink'd Publishing.

•••••••••••••

Angus McIntyre is the author of the space-opera novella "The Warrior Within", published by Tor.com in 2018. His short fiction has appeared in a number of magazines and anthologies. For more information, see his website at https://angus.pw/.

•••••••••••••

Ed Ahern resumed writing after forty odd years in foreign intelligence and international sales. He's had over 500 stories and poems published so far, and eleven books. Ed works the other side of writing at Bewildering Stories where he manages a posse of six review editors, and as lead editor at Scribes Micro.

Juliette Jarabek is a fiction writer, a horror fanatic, and a freak of life and death. Fiction is a miraculous tool to explore questions, joys, and fears considered scandalous and taboo, and that is how she strives to use her work. Through her endless pursuits and curiosities, Juliette aims to explore, educate, and inspire—and her aim is getting better!

Ilan Jones lives in the countryside writing horror stories under the shadow of the mountains near the Salish Sea. His work has appeared in Unstamatic Magazine, Dark Matter Magazine, and PULP. You can find him attempting to use X @mountain_horror.

Tom Paul is a speculative writer from Maryland. He has had paranormal experiences and draws from them in his writing. He worked at NIH and the FDA.

•••••••••••••

C.R. Langille spent many a Saturday afternoon watching monster movies with her mom. It wasn't long before she started crafting nightmares to share with her readers. She is a retired, disabled veteran with a deep love for weird and creepy tales. This prompted her to form Timber Ghost Press in January of 2021. She is an award-winning author, affiliate member of the Horror Writers Association, the DEI Chair for the League of Utah Writers, earned her MFA:

Writing Popular Fiction from Seton Hill University in 2014, and was named Editor of the Year by the League of Utah Writers in 2024.

Nidheesh Samant is a product marketer, writer, soup fanatic and collector of trivia. Nidheesh lives with his family in Mumbai, India. Visit him online: @darthnid on Instagram and X or at https://thedarknetizen.wordpress.com/ on Wordpress.

Winston Malone is a USAF veteran who works professionally as a technical writer and editor. He loves reading and writing speculative fiction, and opened Enchanted Books in New Mexico to promote quality independent writing. You can follow more of his work at storyletter.substack.com, lunarawards.com, and havek.world.

ALSO BY

Take Me There: A Speculative Anthology of Travel

www.ingramcontent.com/pod-product-compliance
Lightning Source LLC
La Vergne TN
LVHW041011150826
845672LV00001B/56

* 9 7 9 8 9 8 7 0 0 4 6 8 5 *